ANGELA D SHELTON

Collapse

Second edition

ISBN: 978-1-957649-17-7

Editing by Deirdre Lockhart at Brilliant Cut Editing
Cover art by Clifford Fryman

This book was professionally typeset on Reedsy.
Find out more at reedsy.com

This novel is not the production of one person, and thus I have many to thank. As a Christian author, I must first thank God for the opportunity to write. My family's support and encouragement are blessings. The American Christian Fiction Writers and Word Weavers critique groups honed my skills. Brilliant Cut Editing refined the final product to make it worthy of reading. My deepest gratitude goes out to all who contributed to this effort, and I dedicate this book to all of them.

Contents

Chapter One

The framed painting oozed peace and tranquility. Jan Worthington wished she could crawl into the canvas and become part of the landscape. Lush green fields where tall grasses waved in the gentle breeze were the center of the piece, but the eye-catcher was the girl on a swing underneath an oak in the painting's corner. Her wide-brimmed purple hat, Jan's favorite color, rippled back with the motion, and with the way her feet flew up into the air, life must be carefree for this child.

Jan reached to touch the picture, longing for it, but even more so, wanting to sit on such a swing in such a place, without a care in the world to pull her back down to earth. This was how her life should have been. But at sixteen, she knew a different life, one that wasn't untroubled or without worry.

The artist in her ached to explore the textures of the paint's ridges. The painter perfectly captured the wind's movement and the swing's momentum with their brushstrokes. She longed to hold a paintbrush again and stroke the canvas with colors and textures.

That wasn't her life anymore, though. Now, chicken coop cleaning, calf wrangling, and not nearly enough parties now overtook her days. She should be cheering the football team to a win this weekend, not searching for food alternatives to replace everything they'd lost.

An elbow to her ribs jerked her out of the picturesque places her mind had gone to. "Hello. Earth to Jan, where are you, Jan?"

Her best friend and next-door neighbor, Renee Boswell, was a great cheer buddy but had no eye for art. With her golden blond hair under a ball cap, and her suntanned arms and face, she looked anything but her German-American heritage.

Chin high, Jan swiped at the red hair poking out of a similar baseball cap, then jammed her hands on her slim hips, her fingers grazing her best market-day jeans and T-shirt. "Can't you even take a minute to appreciate how much work went into this painting?"

"Yes, dear. It's a pretty picture." Renee turned from the painting and craned over the market tables spread along the huge field beside the auction barn. "But we've been standing here for like ten minutes already. The day's a'wastin'."

Jan twitched her lips and let out a breath. "Fine." Turning to the vendor behind the table, she said, "It's an exquisite painting. I love your brushstrokes."

The white-haired man bowed his head in acknowledgment. "It's been a while since I had fresh materials. This was one of the last ones I created before Andy's Art Supply shut down. I hate to part with it, but if you can come up with a pound of that dried beef your mama makes, it's all yours."

An entire pound of dried beef? That wasn't going to happen. Practically a king's ransom these days. But the guy was so skinny, and the artwork was all he had to trade. One day, she would have all the art she wanted in her own place. One day.

She sniffed the air. Normally, the most prominent smell

would be the auction barn. It took a lot to mask its stench, but something nearby smelled sweet. She grabbed her BFF's arm and tugged her toward the smell. "I smell sorghum."

They might be a little too old to be walking arm-in-arm through the market-day tables. But she didn't care. They had once been two of almost a dozen friends who had sleepovers and pillow fights. But most had to move away from Shiloh, Georgia, for their parents to find work.

"I think it's over this way." Renee hauled her down another line of tables, Jan's feet tripping along on the dirt path between the vendors.

Steam rose from an enormous cauldron over a fire. An elderly man stirred the contents with a wooden paddle, his thin gray hair frizzing in the steam. Pint-sized jars gleamed on the table to his right. The dark sorghum syrup would be a sweet addition to their pantry. Giant popcorn balls beckoned from a glass plate.

"Are you making molasses?" Jan asked.

"What do you think they're doing, goofball?"—Renee elbowed her—"their laundry?"

As Jan giggled, the older woman at the table smiled. "Actually, the molasses is already in the container. We're turning it into taffy." She pointed at the row. "The smell always brings people in."

Candy was a rare treat. Since the variants started four years ago, Jan had fewer opportunities for the sweet things in life every year.

Closing her eyes, she breathed in deeply. Just standing here and indulging in smelling it was a treat. "I'm afraid to even ask how much the taffy costs."

The woman dabbed at her forehead, then tucked a handkerchief into her sleeve, and glanced over her shoulder at her husband. Absorbed in his task, he didn't look up.

"Tell you what..." Dropping her voice to a conspiratorial whisper, she winked. "I don't see too many young folks around here anymore. I'll trade you a full bag to share if you can get me a half-dozen jars of fruit. Deal?"

That would have been an excellent trade. But Mom was selling canned vegetables back at their table, not fruit. Mrs. Boswell, Renee's mom, was helping because they had nothing of their own to sell.

"Give us a little while." Her arm still linked through Renee's, Jan gave it a squeeze. "I've got a plan."

"What are you thinking?" Renee, always up for an adventure, asked as they ran together back to their table.

"I'll bet we can trade her some of Dad's dried beef and two jars of spinach."

Dried beef was a delicacy few could afford these days. Their expanding beef farm provided a few steers every year that Dad raised and butchered. Mom would salt and dry much of it for sale on market day.

Back at their table, Mom and Mrs. Boswell were busy with two different customers, negotiating a trade. Mom's thin arms shook as if she needed to sit down before exhaustion overtook her. Even with the white sun hat shading her face, sweat slicked along her hairline while her low-hanging ponytail snaked down the side of her neck onto her bright yellow "lucky" sales shirt.

As soon as Mom finished with her customer, Jan used her very best sad-puppy-dog look. That always worked on Mom. "Can we have a bag of dried beef and two jars of spinach?"

Mom shook her ponytail off her shoulder, the slippery dark strands complying. "What for?"

Jan pinched her BFF's arm to get her attention. This would require a double team effort and help them continue to earn their nickname—Double Trouble.

"Candy?" *Double down on the look and pull hands up into a pleading gesture.*

When Renee joined in, eyes round and sad, Mom laughed. "That's a steep price for a treat. Don't you think?"

No response except for the addition of a quivering lip. If the puppy-dog eyes didn't seal the deal, the quivering lip always did. Never let it be said that Jan didn't know how to sell a deal.

"All right, uncle. I give up," Mom said. "But only this one time. No more. Got it?"

The serious-mom eyes were out and functioning just as well as puppy-dog ones.

"Got it," Jan and Renee chorused.

Mom handed over the package of dried beef and vegetable jars, and off they went. Jan may never become an advertising executive—the whole idea of selling people things they didn't need or want seemed silly now—but nothing would stop her from becoming the best bargainer at the auction. And someday, she'd use her artistic skills to create something people would value as much as food.

«»

On the way home, Jan crammed next to Renee in the truck bed, slowly chewing on their taffy. Once the sorghum seller saw the dried beef, it cemented the sale. Jan hadn't even needed her renowned skills.

The truck jostled over something, and she almost yelped as she bumped against Renee. As she righted herself, glad to have avoided the gooseneck Dad installed to pull the cattle trailer, Caleb gave her a look she'd have stuck her tongue out at if she didn't have candy. Only two years her senior, her brother acted much older and had already resumed his serious expression, blue eyes looking nowhere as if lost in thought. His muscular body, hardened from long hours helping Dad, and handsome features along with Mom's dark hair had young women at the market turning heads. He was always there when she needed him.

With the long folding table behind their backs, she and Renee leaned on it now. Tucked in between them were the remaining unsold items and those things they'd taken in on trade. After such a busy day, not a scrap of the dried beef returned with them.

Mrs. Boswell had made an admirable trade, scoring two-dozen empty canning jars, all with the reusable lids in exchange for only one jar of spinach. Normally, an empty jar was part of the sale price for a full jar of produce, but one rarely found the reusable lids. Now the jars tinkled together as Dad slowed, while he neared potholes, to avoid breaking glass or jostling harder than they already were on the deteriorating roads. She remembered when crews kept the roads smooth as glass. Now, who knew how bad the roads would be next year?

Talked out after the day, Jan just rested her shoulder against Renee's. But it was a comfortable silence. She stretched one leg out, resting it against the back of the cab while beyond the window Renee's parents' animated gestures in the Ram's rear seat seemed to fill the silence even if Jan couldn't hear what they were saying.

Though it was hot, the wind fluttered the length of her ponytail behind her.

The truck slowed at their long driveway. This was the worst part of the ride. Dad hit the end of the driveway where a pothole had developed between the road pavement and the dirt drive. The resulting smack flung their bodies up, then back down—hard.

"Oomph."

About halfway up the driveway, the trees opened to expose their one-hundred-acre Angus beef farm, and a warm feeling of belonging enveloped her.

Once Dad had parked, they disentangled themselves from the cargo and tumbled over the side, since the tongue of the empty trailer prevented their exit via the tailgate.

"Don't leave without taking an armload, ladies." Dad reached in and handed her and Renee each a case of the empty jars. He was always efficient, rarely having to repeat any motions as he worked.

Hugging her case to her chest, Jan smirked. He had to be the most handsome man in the world with a military cut that barely allowed his graying hair to show. At six five, he projected authority without trying.

The smell of the country surrounded them. Cow patties, freshly turned soil, and wildflowers blooming somewhere close, all combined to welcome her home. Heaven.

"Mom, can the Boswells stay for supper?" she asked as her mom stepped through the door in front of her.

"Of course. Let me ask them," Mom responded.

It wouldn't be a fancy dinner, but Jan often worried her friend's family didn't have enough to eat. Mr. Boswell had taken on odd jobs since the store where he worked shut down. The variant Upsilon finished the store off right as it killed billions and caused the world supply chain to splinter irreparably.

The Boswells all appeared thinner than normal today, and Renee had ogled the dried beef they'd traded. Jan cringed. She should've given her friend the beef instead of wasting it on the treats.

After two more trips, along with everyone else, they'd carried everything into the house and followed Mom into the kitchen, the hardwood floors and marble counters cool after the heat outside. Back before the variant, Mom had let Jan help her select the new cabinets and barstools when they modernized the room. Mom had praised her artistic eye, and Jan still savored stepping into the room with its soothing matte blue and subtle recessed lighting.

"Why don't you ladies peel potatoes?" Mom asked.

"Yes, ma'am," Jan responded. When she opened the pantry, only one potato remained. "Guess we're going into the cellar."

She led Renee back outside and around the house to the root cellar door, the windowless, solid cement room creepy even with the dim light she flicked on. Never one to linger down here, she scooted across the room right quick, Renee crowding close.

"Wow." Renee shook open the bag to fill. "That potato bin's a lot lower than last time."

"It's still about a quarter full." Jan flicked away a greedy spider slinking into the bin. "It'll get us through until the fall harvest. But, seriously, let's hurry."

Together they gathered a bag full and toted them back to the kitchen. Jan's family was blessed. Her parents had installed solar panels before the shortages had begun. Back then, they had two large freezers to store their beef. That, combined with frequent power outages in the small town, led them to go solar. A freezer of spoiled meat was such a waste.

Since the outages were common and sometimes lasted for days, theirs was one of the few farms functioning without a hiccup. Having an electric stove, dishwasher, and even air conditioning was living high on the hog these days.

While the men finished evening chores, the four ladies worked in the kitchen. Then Jan headed out to the front porch and rang the dinner bell. No matter where someone was on the farm, they'd hear the bell ring. No one was late for dinner after the bell got rung.

"Set the table, please, ladies," Mom said.

Once everyone sat, she asked for a blessing on the food. "Father, we thank you for another successful day at the market. We also thank you for our dear friends who make each day serving you more joyful. Thank you for this food you give us. Amen."

Amens chorused around the table.

Soon, silverware clacked against plates and serving dishes. The scent of mashed potatoes mingled with the savory beef roast. They rarely enjoyed an entire beef roast. Instead, meat became a flavoring for vegetables and grains because it was so valuable for trade.

Mom must have noticed the weight her neighbors had lost as well. She'd be too polite to say anything, though.

Near the end of the meal, Mr. Boswell tinkled his spoon against his glass. The sound silenced all ongoing discussions. "I've got an announcement to make," he began. "We're going to be moving next week. We're heading to Columbus to look for work."

Jan's stomach fell as if on an express elevator to the basement. "What?" she shrieked. "No! You can't leave. Why can't you find work here?"

"Jan." Dad had The Look on his face. There was no argument after it arrived.

She shut her mouth and her eyes as if not seeing would stop the inevitable. Under the table, she clenched her hands into fists, but there was no physical enemy to fight. She'd been afraid this was coming for weeks now. So many had left the town, looking for better fortunes or at least government support in the larger cities. Market day was becoming sparser each week.

Renee had been her BFF for as long as she could remember. They'd worn a path down between their two houses. Dad had even put gates in the fences so they wouldn't try sliding under the electric wires.

How would she survive without Renee?

She grabbed a hold of her friend's hand under the table and squeezed hard. This might be the last meal where they sat together at this table. Her last friend in the area was going to leave, and she couldn't do anything about it. She hated the changes the wretched variant caused to her world, the things it had stolen from her. These last years, she'd tried so hard to put on a smile, to cheer everyone up. But no pep rally could cheer her through this.

Tears rolled down her cheeks, and when she opened her eyes, she wasn't alone in shedding them.

Chapter Two

"Ow... Stop... My finger's stuck!" Jan bobbled in place but continued to hold the net taut against her brother's pull.

"Okay, hold on." Caleb loosened his grip so she could extract her gloved finger.

Her finger free, she once again tightened her hold while he completed the heavier lift. With the net across the top of the chicken run, they attached it to the corner poles. While he had the harder task, her muscles still strained to keep the net taut for him to finish the job. After years of farmstead work, she'd grown strong enough to keep up.

"You can let go now. I've got it," he said.

Relieved, she dropped the netting and removed her glove. Red and swollen, her finger throbbed. Whew, no significant damage.

"If you'd pay attention more, you wouldn't get hurt all the time. Quit daydreaming and focus." His stoic face told her he was in work mode. The same look Dad carried every day. When had he turned into Dad?

She glared back. Arguing would be pointless. She picked up the tools and supplies. With the pounding in her finger slowing her, she fumbled not to tangle it again.

"Your finger okay?" His tone calmer, he bent to help with the cleanup.

"Fine. What's next?"

The chores never ended. That was the nature of farmwork.

When her parents bought the old broken-down farm, they'd all struggled to restore it. She'd resented the long workdays consuming her weekends and the daily chores after school. Now she loved the land that had not only been the answer to her parents' dreams but also a necessity.

"I need to go help Dad round up the cows for their vaccines. Why don't you help Mom in the greenhouse? And stay on your toes. You know you need to do the heavy lifting for Mom. But you have to think of it before she does. Right?"

Ugh, blah, blah, bossy, blah.

"You don't have to remind me all the time."

"I wouldn't if you'd focus."

She stuck her tongue out.

"Mature... real mature," he said.

Who wanted to be mature? She smirked. "Don't let Tony stomp your foot."

She stalked toward the greenhouse, and chickens scattered out of her way. Only the bull caused her brother to pause. At well over 2,500 pounds, Tony could inflict permanent damage with a flick of his enormous head. Jan avoided being in his vicinity. Caleb had no choice.

Time to hoof it to the greenhouse since they no longer used the ATV to travel around the farm. Sweat beads popped out on her forehead, and her shirt stuck to her back, damp with perspiration.

She missed driving the vehicle. She missed a lot of things, especially her friends. In kindergarten, she amassed friendships and had only added to those throughout her school years. Since the buses stopped running, those relationships dropped out of her life.

Maybe I'll try to email Renee tonight. I'll bet she's fit to be tied.

Who could go a whole month without talking to her best friend? Well, who other than Caleb. Besides, Renee had to be going nuts, stuck in an apartment with her cousins instead of free in the country.

Best to focus, as Caleb said.

The pain in the butt was right sometimes.

A breeze caught Jan's hat and lifted it up on her forehead, chilling the sweat on her body for a wonderful second. She sprinted the last fifty yards to the greenhouse between the hay and equipment barns. Its door rattled, and her mother, gloved hands deep into the coco coir potting mix, huffed a damp black tendril away from her eyes. "What's the rush?"

"Don't want to be out in the heat too long today, right?" Jan ducked into the steamy building and peered over her mother's shoulder.

She'd put the water in with the compressed bale the night before, leaving the mixture light and airy today, perfect for sowing the seeds in the hydroponic system. Having a private well with a solar-powered pump allowed them to maintain their system long after others abandoned theirs. Growing food year-round kept them fed and healthy.

"What are you planting today?" Jan breathed in long and deep, the smell of earth and water invigorating her, making her feel as if she'd put down roots. At this hour, the heat in here remained bearable. She needed to get the planting done fast to beat it.

Mom no longer had the stamina to work in the heat. Still,

being a headstrong woman, she'd work until exhaustion hit. Dad had to help her back into the cool farmhouse more than once.

"We're planting romaine lettuce today. We still have time for one last crop before we start plants for the garden." Mom's yellow sun hat bore globs of potting soil, and perspiration darkened her gray T-shirt. "It isn't your favorite, but we used up this season's Bibb seeds."

Jan stepped up to the potting mix's five-gallon bucket. "Let me see that."

As her mother backed away, Jan hefted the container onto the bench for easier reach. She then pulled a stool out from under the shelf supporting the system and slid it next to her mother. The soil container on the work ledge a bit above Jan's waist almost reached her petite mother's chest. However, the stool put her in a better position.

"There. Now you can sit on the stool." Jan patted it and edged in beside it. "We can make an assembly line. I'll fill the pots, and you'll plant the seeds."

Mom crossed her arms over her chest. "I don't need to sit down."

"It's easier to work at the height of the stool because the bucket is so high, isn't it?"

"Just pass me a pot." Huffing, her mother maneuvered onto the seat.

For the next thirty minutes, Jan filled the four-inch containers with coco coir, and her mother placed the tiny seeds, careful to give them the best chance to sprout. Jan's speed kept Mom busy and allowed Jan to grab the pots her mother seeded and fit them into the system's tubes.

With the task completed, she topped off the reservoir water

while her mother measured the solution's nutrients.

Wiping her hands on her jeans, her mother grinned. "That sure went fast. What has you rushing through the work?"

Jan winked. "I wanted to give you time to make muffins if you were thinking of using those blueberries up."

Mom laughed. "Oh, I see how it is now. You aren't planning your day—you're planning mine."

Her ploy successful, Jan ushered her mother toward the air-conditioned house. As her heart ached, she averted her gaze from Mom's sweaty hair clinging to her already sagging shoulders.

Extreme temperatures weakened her ability to do outdoor work—something she'd never admit or give in to. Jan stayed with her mother until they were safe inside and her mother sat on a kitchen stool with a glass of ice water.

She'd gotten sick with a variant early on when people still called it COVID-19. Having spent a month in the hospital and a week on a ventilator, she was fortunate to have survived. Now she had the long variant syndrome but could get around without oxygen. With the once-common gas, as well as parts for the portable machines making oxygen, in short supply, only the wealthy could afford such treatments.

While her mother rested, Jan rummaged through ingredients from the walk-in pantry. "How about I get the batter started? They turned out pretty good when I made them last time."

But that would be too easy, and Mom never took it easy.

"Nope. I'm ready." She shooed Jan toward the door. "Go see if your father and Caleb need help."

«»

The heat of the day accentuated the cow-patty scent as Jan approached the corral. By the end of the day, all three of them would smell of dung. Her nose scrunched. Hopefully, she wouldn't be covered in it as well.

"Come on over here and start prepping the shots, Jan." Dad already had muck on his shirt from slapping the rear ends of the cattle being corralled into the chutes. A look similar to Caleb's firmed his face. Work mode. No fooling around permitted.

With the ankle-deep grass outside of the fencing lush and green today, some of the larger cattle poked heads under the gates, tongues reaching for the fresh food. The hills in the distance held her fascination, calling her to find her friend and explore the woods—like that could happen.

Nope. Focus. Work to do.

She sidestepped a thistle on her way, then opened the cooler on the truck's lowered tailgate. Ignoring the fly spray and water jugs on Dad's makeshift table, she attached needles to syringes and clamped the first tag into the plier set. Caleb and Dad lined up the cattle in the alley and corral boxes.

The truck, fulfilling its role as a table, rarely moved. Since the coronavirus struck in 2019, business interruptions accelerated to the point of severe shortages. As gas had become a luxury few could afford every day, the fuel shortage changed the world. When the internet still worked, schools went online for anyone not within walking distance. People crowded into the cities to avoid expensive commutes. Those who'd bought electric vehicles while they were available drove—if they had electricity to charge them.

Her parents installed solar at the farm as one of their first improvements. The old farmhouse barely held up the panels, but they'd shored her up to handle the weight.

"All set, Jan?" her father asked. With her nod, he yelled into the corral over the herd's lowing and bellowing. "Send the first ones through, Caleb."

The alley door opened, and the column of cows and calves started toward the chute. As the first cow's head came through, Dad closed the catch around her neck and activated the squeezing mechanism. After her father completed the injections, Caleb applied the fly treatment. Though such vaccines were scarce worldwide, the local vet had procured enough for the nearby farmers this season. Unfortunately, this might be the last time they could vaccinate the herd.

After they verified and documented the cow's tag, Dad released its sides. He freed her head next, and the young mama bolted into the holding pen. They processed the next six cows and heifers.

When a young male arrived at the end of the chute, Dad held up a hand. "We're keeping this one separated for finishing. Let's get the herd back into the field."

With the two heftier steers penned away from the herd, they'd fatten them up on an expensive meal mixture of corn, cottonseed meal, and oats.

Jan followed her father and Caleb into the pen. They staked out their zones, having worked this process many times. When Dad opened the pasture gate, the small herd ran to the pen's edges and circled the end. She and Caleb moved behind the group, hands raised and calling, "Yaw! Out you go. Move it. Come on."

Their herd had grown to fifty-two animals counting the calves, cows, heifers, steers, and Tony the bull. They'd need the entire day to care for all the animals.

They returned to the young steer. Jan handed Dad the vaccines while Caleb prepped the fly spray applicator. After her father stepped away, Caleb applied the liquid to the steer's back. The steer shook his head up and down and kicked the chute's rear door.

"Aren't you a little high-headed today?" Her dad rubbed the steer's head, causing even more of a ruckus as the animal tried to free itself. "Step back, Caleb. This one's cranky."

When the squeezing mechanism released, the kicking increased. Dad freed the steer's head, and the animal jumped and ran into the open pen, kicking up his hindquarters and snorting.

"What's gotten into him?" Jan swiped at her brow with her sodden shirt. "He has a tag, so he's been through this before." She'd have to check his tag number in the records to see if he was high-headed last fall. If his mama produced high-headed calves, they'd need to sell her.

"Not sure, but he's got a bee in his bonnet today." Dad paused, hands on hips, then shook his head as if dismissing an idea. "Let's get him into the feeding pen."

As he opened the feeding pen, Jan and Caleb circled to the steer's rear to push him.

"Move it, forty-seven. Let's go!" Caleb called out to get the steer's attention and crowded the critter, with her help to draw the steer into a smaller and smaller area.

Then the animal charged in the opposite direction, bolting around Caleb.

"Oh, come on." Jan's initial adrenaline spike at the animal's charge turned to frustration at having to start the corralling process over again. Once again, they circled behind the animal to herd it toward the open gate.

"Quit being stubborn. Just go into the pen and get your treats." Too bad she didn't have a bucket handy. Most of the herd associated a rattling bucket with treats, and the temptation usually lured them into the desired area.

Without the bucket, words alone did not affect number 2347. As they approached, he continued to toss his head and look wild-eyed at them, pacing back and forth, seeking an escape path.

"Yaw! Into the pen." Caleb advanced on the steer.

Jan screeched as the steer charged her brother.

Shoot, not that way!

Her heart thundered in her chest while the adrenaline ramped up.

"Caleb!" Dad got out the warning before the animal ran over Caleb, knocking him to the ground.

Caleb lay there, unmoving.

Chapter Three

"Caleb! Caleb!" Jan screamed as she ran to her brother, the frantic steer forgotten. As she dropped to her knees at Caleb's side, her heart stuttered. She struggled to draw her next breath. He lay still with blood oozing from his head, a red-stained stone beside his ear. The coppery scent wafted to her nose, making her want to vomit. "Dad!"

Her father hadn't forgotten the crazed animal and was keeping it from rounding back to where Caleb lay.

"Dad!" Yes, he had to get the steer safely away first, but fear surged through her.

He walked toward the yearling again, arms waving above his head. As it ran into the feeding lot, Dad slammed the gate, closing the animal in. Then he sprinted to Caleb and dropped to his knees to inspect the damage.

First, a pulse check, then a hand to the chest. Relief flooded her father's eyes, and he bowed his head briefly.

"He's breathing."

She reached for her brother to shake him awake, but her father grabbed her hand.

"Don't touch him. We don't know if it's safe to move him yet. Let me look." He eased aside the hair on Caleb's scalp, inspecting the bloody mess as the red ooze dripped off Caleb's ear.

Jan's heart pounded against her ribs. She knelt on her hands to keep them from interfering with her father's work.

An eternity passed before her father caught her eye. "I need you to run to the house and grab the first aid kit." The calm voice he used scared her more than if he'd yelled at her. "Don't burst into the house and upset your mom, though. We don't need her trying to come out here. Just get the kit and get back here as quick as you can."

"Yes, sir." Jan jumped to her feet and sprinted toward the house. She spun back as Caleb let out a moan. His eyes opened into slits, and he tried to roll over.

"Just lie there for a minute, son. You took a beating." Dad looked back at her. "Go."

She took off running as fast as she could in her clunky steel-toed boots. But who could move fast in the safety footwear they wore around the cattle?

She clambered up the front steps out of breath, her chest heaving. Needing to get her breathing under control so Mom wouldn't know something was up, she paused at the door and took slow, deep, calming breaths. In—one, two, three. Out—one, two, three. After a few of these, though not entirely normal, she could fake peace.

Everything is fine. There are no problems. It's all good.

With that calming recitation in her head, she opened the door and removed her boots in the mudroom. She entered the kitchen where Mom was cleaning up as the muffins baked. The aroma of blueberries, vanilla, and sorghum overwhelmed Jan's senses and tempted her to relax, but she stiffened her spine. "Smells amazing, Mom."

"You on another break already?"

"Have to stop in the bathroom. I guess I drank too much water before I started."

She added a smile and then darted to the bathroom. Thankfully, they kept small first aid kits in each bathroom and larger ones in their get-out-of-Dodge bags if they had to run. The small one had better do since she could get it out of the house discreetly. She flushed the toilet to keep up appearances and then stuck the kit under her shirt at the small of her back and tucked the shirt in to keep it secure. She kept her back turned away from her mom to hide the bulge as she passed through the kitchen.

"I've got a batch cooling if you want to take one for yourself, Dad, and Caleb."

Really? Now? She needed to get back to Caleb.

She edged sideways toward the door to get out without looking suspicious.

"Thanks, but we're already pretty filthy." She left the room, calling back. "You know how it goes."

"Ah, yes." Mom spoke louder as Jan moved further away. "I remember, even though it's been a while. I'll hold a warm batch aside for when you finish. Ice-cold milk is waiting."

"Yum, can't wait." She reached for her boots and fumbled them on, leaving the laces untied. "Later, Mom."

After she shut the door, she sprinted across the meadow. When she arrived, Caleb was sitting up with his hand pressed to his head.

What a relief.

"Here." She shoved the kit at her father.

He opened the kit, removed a bottle of alcohol, and uncapped it. "I need to pour some alcohol on the wound, Caleb. Move your hand. It's going to sting." He peeled Caleb's fingers away and then poured the bottle over the bloody area, lifting the hair as he went.

"Agrh!" Caleb moaned and craned his head backward.

Stress ebbed from her body. Caleb's complexion had regained a normal pink.

Dad then pulled out a sterile bandage and placed it on the wound. He secured it with sterile gauze, then taped the ends.

"Keep some pressure on it, son, to stop the bleeding. You're going to have a headache for a while, but that's probably the worst of it. It doesn't look like you need any stitches. How are you feeling?"

"Think I'm going to puke," Caleb said.

Dad pointed toward the truck back at the chute system. "Go get us a bottle of water, Jan."

After she collected the water with as much speed as she could muster and handed it over, he opened it for Caleb. "Drink a little. If you keep it down, we'll get you up and to the house."

Caleb closed both hands over the bottle and sipped. "Sorry, Dad. I didn't mean to slow us down today. Just give me a minute, and I'll be ready to go."

"Not going to happen today. You scared me there. Losing consciousness isn't something to take lightly. We need to get you checked out by a professional before you go back to work."

"No!" Caleb's eyes grew wide as his head shot up. He winced and closed his eyes with a moan. "I'm fine. We don't need to waste fuel."

"Your health is more important than some gasoline." Dad clamped a hand on Caleb's shoulder.

"Dad, I'm fine," Caleb insisted.

Jan jigged from foot to foot, her heart rate kicking up again. She wanted to be sure Caleb was safe, but he was right. They had to sell off four steers to secure fuel last year. With gas so scarce, they avoided using it except for critical tasks, such as moving the hay bales into the fields with the tractor. They rarely tilled new soil, manually working as much as they could. No one knew if they'd be able to secure any more when their 250-gallon tank ran dry. Then they might have to harvest hay by hand, as the Amish did. Maintaining a herd of cows then would be difficult.

Dad stood and held his beefy hand out to Caleb. "Let's get you up if you think you can now."

Taking the proffered hand, Caleb rose. He wobbled a bit and then stood firm, head held high, but his complexion paled again. "See, I'm up. It's all good."

"Good. So, we can go down the road to Doc Henderson instead of into Columbus."

Caleb shook his head but stopped with a pained look—the movement changed to a slow and brief nod.

Thank goodness, he was up and moving. It couldn't be too bad, right?

Columbus, a forty-five-minute drive away, was home to the closest remaining hospital with a medical staff. That would eat a decent chunk of their fuel supply. Alternatively, many farmers stopped in for minor injuries at Doc Henderson's office, the local vet. Proficient with human stitches, the vet could also provide X-rays and simple fracture care. If Doc couldn't do what needed to be done, he'd refer you to the larger facility. Their family was fortunate to have the fuel to get to the hospital if required, but Jan prayed they wouldn't have to.

"Let's get you into the truck. Jan, run back down to the house, and we'll meet you there. Tell Mom Caleb needs to see Doc, but he's all right. Then meet us at the front door."

As she ran, her legs wobbling, she rehearsed ways to tell Mom what happened. When she came into the kitchen, her mother slid another batch of muffins out of the oven. "Hey, Mom. You'll need to turn off the oven for now. Caleb got hurt, and we're taking him to see Doc. He's okay, though."

"What happened?" Mom's eyes went wide as she threw off the stained oven mitts. The muffin tin clattered to the counter.

"Just hit his head on a rock, I think. A steer knocked him over. But Dad wants to be sure."

While Mom ran to the front door, Jan switched off the oven and joined her as the truck lumbered down the hill.

They drove three miles to the vet's office, then waited their turn to have Caleb's wounds evaluated. The vet agreed with Caleb. With no permanent damage, he needed to take it easy for a couple of days—but no need to travel to Columbus.

Relieved, Jan elbowed him lightly on their way out. "Ready for round two with the steer?"

"Ha. I heard you scream like a girl when he was coming our way."

She rolled her eyes. "That's because I am a girl."

Caleb gave her a firm shove, making her stumble. She wouldn't push back—this time. Man, goofing around again felt good.

On the way home, they passed a man trudging alongside the road. He hunched forward, the heavy load of a backpack almost three-quarters of his size weighing him down. Sweat glistened on his arms and face.

Jan scooted forward and touched Dad's shoulder. "Stop. Let's give him a ride. He looks exhausted."

"You know the rules, kiddo. We don't know who we can trust."

That sucked. "We can let him ride in the truck bed. There are four of us. What's he going to do? C'mon."

In response, her father sped up.

She crossed her arms over her chest with a huff and slouched back in her seat. "When I've got my own place, I'm going to let anyone who needs help come and live with me. I hate that we can't help them all."

"I'd love to help him. We do help others. But we can't save everyone. If we tried, we might lose what we've worked so hard to gain. You don't understand this now, but you will someday. You can't trust everyone you see."

Jan scowled at her hands and fiddled with her shirt hem, flicking a finger along the butterfly print long ago stained by their land's red dust. *I'm so tired of this same fight, every single time. Sure, we don't have a lot, but we have enough to share. Not everyone wants to steal what we have.*

Why was it that, while she wanted to believe humanity was good at its core, her father wanted to believe the opposite? Once the fuel ran out, they could use help to maintain the farm. Having others on their team would be a good thing. But proving that to Dad? Ha! When the time came, she'd show him, and then he'd have to agree.

Chapter Four

Jan awoke to sizzling potatoes, mooing cows, and clattering food prep. She snuggled in deeper to her duvet, savoring the heaven-on-earth breakfast scent, then wiggled upright, stuck her feet over the edge of her twin daybed, and opened her eyes. The purply walls—matched to the exact hue of ripe clover—still made her smile, recalling memories of her and Renee picking the paint. She yawned again. She missed brewing coffee's earthy smell. How could something that smelled so good taste so horrible? At least, that's how she remembered it.

After hopping out of bed in her early riser mode, she wiggled into jeans, a work shirt, and thick socks to keep her work boots snug in place all day. Once she'd tightened her red hair into a ponytail, she slapped on her hat and trundled down the stairway for breakfast. Mom's whispered prayers mingled with the sizzle from the frying pan. Hearing Dad's name come up, Jan pause before entering the kitchen.

"... and, God, please be with Steve today. I know he still remembers you, even though he's angry. Forgive him his resentment and help him remember the good you've provided and not only the evil he witnessed."

Feeling like a spy, Jan cleared her throat to alert her mother. As she turned the corner, she beamed a sleepy-morning grin and inhaled the savory greasy scent.

"Morning, sweetie." Mom finished the potatoes to prepare to scramble the eggs. "Did you sleep well?"

"I had the most amazing dream. I was back at the school football field. It was game day. All my friends were there, and we had a blast teasing each other and cheering for the team. We were so going to win." She drew in a slow breath to loosen the ache in her chest. Such sweet memories to enjoy in dreams but miss in real life. What she wouldn't give to join the girls for some cheer stunts.

"I know it's hard for you without your friends." Mom swept a strand of black hair from her face before pouring the frothy eggs into the sizzling pan. "But I can't imagine this will last forever. Things will turn around someday. They have to."

Dad came into the kitchen next and scooped Jan up. "Grr... The bear is going to squish you with his love." With his massive arms wrapped around her, he pulled her off her feet into his chest. He ran his rough beard over her neck, grumbling deep in his throat. Jan giggled like she was five again and struggled to break free until tears of laughter streamed down her face. Only then did he place her on her feet and step back so she could recover.

Caleb walked in, grinning at them. He punched her on the arm as he passed by. "Morning, Squirt."

Resenting the nickname that reminded her daily she was younger, smaller, and sometimes less capable of the hard farm chores, she stuck her tongue out.

As Caleb approached his father, they threw fake punching jabs and clapped each other on the shoulder. Their traditional morning greeting.

They were such a good team running the farm, and Caleb

wanted to be just like Dad. She'd catch him mimicking their father's movements without even knowing he was doing it.

"We working on the east pasture today?" Caleb got right down to business. She hadn't seen her brother get the bear-hug treatment since he'd declared himself too old for "sissy stuff" when he turned thirteen.

"That's what I figured." Dad filled a glass of water. "If we're going to add another batch of heifers to the herd in May, we'll need additional grazing area. Of course, you're going to take it slow today. We don't want to overwork you until we know you're solid. That steer hit shook you pretty well."

"I'm fine—"

Dad's raised eyebrow ended Caleb's argument.

Each season, they'd gotten another pasture's fences cleared and repaired so they could add to the number of animals the farm could support. The individual zones had been untended for so long, most of the wires dangled and couldn't hold electrical currents to contain the herd. Saplings grew up along them, and old trees had died and fallen across them, leading to a lot of fence clearing before they started repairs.

"Today is washing day, so make sure you get your baskets into the laundry room before you take off for the field, Caleb," Mom said. "You too, Jan."

"I was planning to pick peas again this morning." Jan set the plates on the table, wanting to make sure everyone knew she wouldn't be in the house today. It was too beautiful a day for staying inside and cleaning.

"We'll drop you off on our way out." Dad snitched a mini muffin from Mom's tray.

Jan held back an eye roll. The pea patch was in the back corner of their property, well away from the house or the pasture the men would work today. He wanted to drop her off, not to save her steps, but to make sure the area was safe before she started working.

Though he rarely spoke of his military career, Mom had explained so they'd understand his overly protective actions. He'd learned to clear an area of all potential enemies before troops entered and set up camp. Even fifteen years later, Jan still saw him clear the house every time they came home. While it annoyed her each time he cleared an area for her, she did her best to suppress the feeling and respect his need to do it.

"Let's eat," Mom announced, and once everyone had sat down, they bowed their heads for her to give the blessing. "Father, we thank you for this food we are about to enjoy. We're so blessed to have so much when many go hungry. Please protect us all today as we go about our jobs. In Jesus's name, we pray. Amen."

Mom always asked the blessings before meals. Though Dad rarely spoke of God, Mom told her children that his faith had faltered when he was in the military. But he never objected to Mom's continued faith. The events he'd witnessed and taken part in stuck with him. Although Mom said she continued to pray his faith would return, his relationship with God remained distant. Yet, by bowing for these prayers, it seemed Dad acknowledged God existed while ignoring Him in muted anger. Tit for tat, so to speak. Stalemate. Would he ever give in and accept what happened, then move on?

While Jan enjoyed the scrambled eggs and potatoes, her favorite was the blueberry muffin she indulged in last. The rich, moist berry with hints of molasses sang a song on her tongue and brought joy to her stomach. Crunchy bits of pecan, harvested from their orchard, added texture to the exquisite delight. The small things in life were good. She missed the taste of cinnamon, though. Mom used that now-scarce spice just a few years ago when the world still stocked grocery store shelves and Jan's biggest worry had been getting good grades and practicing the newest routines with the girls—and hoping health authorities didn't cancel the game.

With cleanup finished, they headed to the golf cart. The ATV would have provided more room, but they rarely used the gas hog. Today, they needed the electric cart to drag around tools and fence-repair supplies. Dad charged the cart from the solar batteries through the house's outside outlets. But they still used it sparingly to keep it running as long as possible since parts were nonexistent.

"There isn't a lot of room in the back today, Jan, but if you hold the tool kit in your lap, you'll fit," Dad said.

Jan wiggled in around the two fence posts laid across the middle of the second-row seat and positioned her feet on either side of the spools of wire on the floor. A bucket of spare parts and a tool bag faced her. She lifted the tool bag, then the bucket. Sure enough, though it was heavy, the tool bag weighed less than the bucket. She crawled into the seat and hefted the bag onto her lap. Once she called out that she was ready, they trundled across the field.

Because her lap was full, Caleb was the designated gate attendant. Each time they crossed into a new pasture, he climbed out to open the gate and close it after the cart drove through. Stopping at each enclosure slowed their pace, but Jan relaxed, breathed the fresh morning air, and enjoyed the scenery.

While they'd eaten, the sun had come up, and birds now flitted by, chirping. Chickens had wandered into the cow pastures and picked their way through the fields, eating bugs off the cow patties. Jan tipped her face toward the sun and closed her eyes to drink in the warmth, still pleasant this early, stifling a groan when they arrived at the backfield.

She disentangled herself from the tool bag and gathered up her bucket. While she clambered past thistles and budding plants over to the first row, Dad drove a circle around the garden area, looking into the woods surrounding the field.

How could security be so important?

They were miles from the closest inhabited house and on well-marked land with no-trespassing signs. With a driveway a half-mile long, she only saw people these days when they got into the truck and went somewhere.

Finally, he circled back. "If you hear anything suspicious, you hightail it back home without waiting to investigate. Right?"

"Yes, sir."

"Okay. Love you. Be safe and enjoy the day."

Dad and Caleb drove off, heading for their work area as she wandered over to where she'd left off last time. On such a warm, blue-skied day, the wildflowers around the garden released sweet fragrance. She stooped and gathered red clover flowers to create a bouquet. Pity, most people ignored their beauty and trampled them.

She sighed. *Better get going, or I'll be out here all day.*

She edged sideways through the deer fence and over to the last row she'd harvested. Then her scalp prickled. Something wasn't right. She'd only picked through the first five long rows of peas, but the last row on the far end looked trampled. How did a deer get through the fence?

Hands on her hips, she scanned the line, not seeing any breaks where one might have gotten in. Moving through the garden, she pressed her lips tight. Something hadn't merely trampled the plants. There were footprints in the dirt where someone had pulled up whole plants. A person had been in the garden—and recently.

Chapter Five

She had to calm down. Dad had scanned the area before he dropped her off, so whoever had been here wasn't here now. Right? She rechecked the field and wood line anyway. Oak, pine, and pecan trees surrounded the entire farm with gardens and pastures carved out of the woods. She'd appreciated the mature trees towering over their land, providing a reprieve from the heat—until now. Anyone could hide in there. Closing her eyes, she took deep breaths the way she'd coached her nervous friends before cheerleading tryouts.

Her heart calmed after a dozen slow inhalations. Opening her eyes, she walked around the uprooted plants and inspected the damage. Huh. She stopped to trace an outline. The shoe prints were small, like hers. Either a child or a petite woman had left them. Her size-seven tracks were more prominent, but not by much.

Calmed even further, she rooted her feet to the land. No need to run off and tell Dad. She'd be safe around a child or woman.

Why would someone pull plants out instead of picking the peas if they wanted some? It made little sense. And they closed the fencing. Did they care about keeping the deer out? Or did the thief think no one would notice? What a strange combination of caring and not caring.

If I tell Dad, I'll never figure out who is doing this. This may be the friend I've been wanting. Now I can prove we don't need to fear strangers.

After she picked the ripe peas, she hummed a tune while she walked back to the house. She might have a friend again soon.

«›»

That evening, Jan entered the dining room barefoot, fresh from the shower. Her wet hair clung to her neck, carrying a hint of homemade peppermint soap. She flicked her red locks over her shoulder and hurried to take a serving dish from Mom.

Mom put food on the table, including some fresh peas Jan shelled earlier. "How did the fence work go today?"

Dad plopped into the chair at the head of the table, the wicker legs scraping against the area rug. Since hardwood floors were easily cleaned from the red Georgia dirt they tracked inside, Mom selected small area rugs in reddish brown hues to "homey up" the living and dining rooms. "We should have that fence up and running again within a few days. The damage wasn't as bad as I'd feared." He took a swig from his water glass. "The high-tinsel wire there is still in relatively good shape, and we could restretch a lot. That last roll of replacement wire might go back into storage for the next repair."

"What a wonderful blessing." Mom squeezed his shoulder before moving to her seat. "It may be the last roll in the entire county at this point."

"Caleb," Dad hollered. "What's keeping you? I'm a hungry man."

A voice yelled back from upstairs, accompanied by thunder-ing stomps on the stairs. "Coming!" Caleb jogged in. "Let's eat."

After Mom prayed for a blessing, they dug into the modest

meal of peas, cornbread, and pinto beans seasoned with some ground beef.

Halfway through, Dad spoke again. "How close to being done is the pea patch, Jan?"

"I'm only about halfway through the rows, but a lot of buds are still coming out. There may be enough to can more next week. I can work it every day at this point."

"Okay. You can take gardening duty while we finish the fencing. Then Caleb and I can help finish harvesting."

"I can handle it, Dad. No problem." She slunk against the backrest of her metal chair, its cool embrace as soothing as the pale walls and crisp clean lines of Mom's décor. If he or Caleb came out, her plan wouldn't work.

Her father's eyebrows arched. "You don't want help? Who are you, and what have you done with my daughter?"

She twisted her lips and raised her eyebrows to mimic him. "Ha ha. I'm laughing on the inside."

Then she sipped from her glass and finished her sales pitch. "If you drop me off every morning for the next week, I can get everything picked on time, and then we'll can what's left after meals. Sound good, Mom?"

Mom let out a small puff of air and relaxed back in her chair, her slim frame seeming to melt into the wicker back and arms. "Thank you, sweetie. I appreciate your help to get it all harvested. That's quite a chore."

Jan smiled back, her heart dancing. Everything was falling into place.

«»

When they rumbled out in the golf cart the next morning, Jan had tucked something extra in her pocket. A brief note, a paper clip, and the nub of a pencil. Before she'd come down for

36

breakfast, she'd composed her greeting.

To Whoever Pulled Out the Pea Plants:

I'm Jan, and the plants you pulled out belong to my family. We don't mind sharing, but please don't pull them out by the roots. If you leave them in the ground, the buds will grow new peas. Then there will be even more to eat and share.

I'd love to meet you in person. Every morning this week, I'll be here. Come on out after my dad and brother leave.

I can't wait!

Jan

Once her father dropped her off, she inspected the new row of plants unearthed at the end of the garden. If this didn't stop soon, Dad would notice the missing plants. She took the note and pencil and secured both to the fence with the clip. Hopefully, whoever was pulling up the plants would see it. Then she got to work and walked back to the house after she finished, skipping part of the way. It was going to be a great week!

«»

The next morning, she dressed so quickly she put her shirt on backward and inside out and groaned when she combed her red hair by the mirror and saw the garment tag under her chin. After right-siding her top, she rushed through the remaining morning ablutions, then dashed to the kitchen, and found it empty. A peek at the microwave showed it was still an hour before breakfast. So much for her internal clock.

With no reason to waste time and too much energy to sit and wait, she gathered ingredients and cooked some fried potatoes to go with scrambled eggs. The sounds of the diced veggies hitting sizzling lard in the pan brought her mother out of the den her parents converted to a downstairs bedroom when Mom first got sick.

"Breakfast cooking already? What got you going so early this morning? Not that I'm complaining. I love having someone cook for me."

"Woke up early. Thought I'd help since I couldn't sleep."

Dad and Caleb wandered in, and they all sat to start the day together.

"Good potatoes, Jan," Dad said. "Nice and crispy, the way I like them."

She wrinkled her nose back at him.

"I'm going to need you to help us with the fences today."

Her spine stiffened, and she stopped chewing. "But I need to harvest the peas while they're still crispy. They taste best when they're young." She couldn't think of any other argument to sway him.

"One or two days won't hurt anything."

"Two days? But, Dad..." His stony expression—the one she and Caleb knew well and called "The Look"—silenced her.

She balled her fists at her side. Not fair. This would ruin the plan.

How else could she get out of the fence work? Her new friend may await her in the pea patch.

All day, she helped trim back tree branches along the fence line, cut down weeds and brambles, and hold tools and wires for the men. Thankfully, all the posts were solid since Dad and Caleb had already replaced any broken or weak ones.

The entire time, all she could think of was the pea patch and the note.

After the longest day of her life, at the supper table, Dad announced they wouldn't need her after all the next day. He hoisted his water glass and winked at her. "I've never seen you clear brush so fast before. You must have had a buzz of energy going on. Maybe you should get up early every day."

Adrenaline shot through her. She dug her toes into the rug and smiled while doing her best to look calm. "Okay. Sounds good. I'll head back to the pea patch in the morning then."

«»

When Jan arrived at the patch, she could barely stand to watch her father ride the golf cart around the garden perimeter, checking the wood line. She held her breath, hoping he wouldn't see anyone but someone would be there, lurking behind the trees, to meet her. Finally satisfied, Dad waved to her and drove off.

She rushed into the fenced-in area to inspect the end where someone had pulled up plants. The note was missing—no response. But no one had uprooted more plants. Instead, someone had picked the peas in the next row, damaging nothing.

She almost whooped. The note had worked.

The golf cart's whir had faded, and she'd given it a few extra minutes to be sure. Then she took a chance.

"Hello? Is anyone out there?" She spoke toward the woods closest to the highway on their property's west side.

No response.

"Anyone? Don't be afraid. I just want to meet you."

Silence.

Her heart sunk. She'd missed her chance because she wasn't here as promised. After scanning one more time, she dropped down by a row to harvest. Perhaps tomorrow she'd meet the person.

Her bucket was close to full when a twig snapped. Jolting, she jumped to her feet from her kneeling position. On the edge of the woods stood a young boy, probably eight or nine years old.

And her whole body sagged. Not a girlfriend, after all. She already had a brother who was a pain in the butt.

As the boy moved closer, making eye contact, she could see how skinny he was, how dirty his face and clothes and dark-red hair were. And something tight clutched at her chest. She smiled as wide and friendly as she could. "Hi there."

"You write the note?" He'd reached the other side of the deer fence now and ogled her bucket.

"Yes, that was me. Sorry I couldn't be here yesterday. I had to help my dad and brother."

He shrugged. "I didn't pull any more out, like you said."

"Perfect." When she walked closer, he jigged a half step back and stopped, so she paused and put a hand up to wave. Lame. "I'm Jan. What's your name?"

"Jacob." He swiped at his nose with his shirt sleeve.

"Do you want to come in and pick more peas, Jacob? Do you have someone to help you?" She held out the bucket for him to see it was close to full.

He shrugged again, walked around to the fence opening, then stepped into the garden. Though inside the enclosure, he stayed close to the exit, so she held out the bucket. Reaching as far as his arms allowed, he pulled a few pods out and chewed on them. "I'm hungry. You got any food?"

He was so young to be alone. How was he surviving?

"Why don't you come back to my house? You can have a hot lunch with my family. Maybe even a hot shower while we wash those clothes."

He kicked a stone from the path. "You sure your family would be okay with that?"

"My mom is a Christian. She'd never turn you away." Dad,

however...

"More peas? I can eat here." He popped open a pod and scraped the peas out with his teeth. With his red hair, he could be mistaken for her little brother—although any brother of hers would be clean.

"No silly. My mom will make you something hot for lunch. Maybe some soup with cornbread."

"Cornbread?" His eyes crinkled. "'K."

"Let's go." She started to grasp his shoulder, but he skittered out of range.

No touching. Got it.

When they entered the house, Jan yelled out to alert her mother. "I'm back, and we've got company."

Mom exited the bedroom carrying a pair of jeans. The threaded needle she'd been using to mend them dropped and swung like a pendulum when she sighted the boy. "Well, hello there. Where did you come from?"

Jan jumped in before the boy could answer. "His name is Jacob, and he's hungry, Mom. He had some peas out of the garden, but I told him we'd give him a hot lunch."

No more questions, please. Just feed him. She clenched her teeth.

"Of course, we'll feed you. Where are your parents?"

"Dad is dead. Mom left." He scuffled his battered sneakers, leaving a red smear on the hardwood floor. "You have cornbread?"

"Mom's is the best in Talbot County." Jan grinned at her mom.

"Jan, take him to the bathroom so he can clean up before your dad and Caleb get here for lunch." Mom folded aside the jeans, stabbing the needle through them for safekeeping. "I'll get that cornbread ready."

«»

When her father and brother got home, Jan introduced them to Jacob. Both scowled at her and the boy. Her father led Mom into the bedroom, and intense murmurs leaked out. Some fifteen minutes later, they returned to the kitchen.

Smiling brightly at Jacob, Mom said, "Well, let's eat."

As soon as the food was on the table, Jacob grabbed a piece of cornbread with one hand and shoveled vegetable soup into his mouth with the other.

Mom's eyebrows shot up, but then she cleared her throat to get his attention. "Jacob, we normally ask for a blessing before we have lunch. Would you mind pausing to join us in prayer?"

He put the spoon down but kept chewing on the massive bite of cornbread already lodged in his mouth. As soon as Mom said amen, his hands were back on the spoon and shoveling furiously.

Dad's frown deepened, but he ate while the spectacle unfolded. Jacob downed two bowls of soup and two hunks of cornbread before the food ran out. Jan felt terrible there wasn't more.

"You should come out to the pasture with us this afternoon, Jacob," Dad said. "You can help us and work off some of that soup. You'll probably get cramps from eating it so fast."

Jacob's face flushed a bright red as he stared at his empty bowl. "'K."

The rest of the afternoon, Jan shucked peas. When she finished, she set some aside for dinner and put the rest into the refrigerator. There weren't quite enough yet to fill a canner for processing, but by tomorrow night, there would be.

Her mother had been sewing in the bedroom, murmuring

when Jan entered the house, likely praying, and considering the situation, Jan could guess her prayer topics. No one had said anything yet about inviting Jacob, a stranger, for lunch. But a lecture would be forthcoming once Dad was back for the evening.

After supper, he showed Jacob upstairs to the spare bedroom. While Mom gave him one of Caleb's old pajama sets to wear so she could wash his clothes, Dad reentered the living room and eyed Jan. Cringing as if she stood under the laser eyes of a superhero, and she imagined the stare burning through her.

Uh-oh, here it came.

"We need to talk, young lady."

"Yes, sir?" She plunked onto a canvas couch cushion, pressed her back hard against a striped throw pillow, knowing the conversation wouldn't be short, and placed her hands under her thighs to keep from fidgeting. She had to look Dad in the eye. That was the rule. Eye contact was essential when he was speaking to you. It was almost painful to do, though. His frown told the entire story. He didn't need to lecture.

The clock ticking above her head seemed to echo inside her.

"How many times have we discussed strangers and the way to avoid them?" With his hands on his hips, he stared down at her.

"Dad, he's just a kid. Did you see him? He's starving to death." She scooted to the edge of the cushions and lifted both hands in appeal. Pleading wouldn't help, but heat rose in her.

How could he be so heartless?

"And how did you know he was alone? You should have run back to the house or to the pasture to get me. I could have made sure he was safe before you invited him into our home—*our home, Jan*." His emphasis meant he was nearing the edge of anger.

She wiggled, every bit of her crying out to argue. But Dad was on a precipice. If she pushed him any further, it could get ugly. Time to apologize.

"I'm sorry. I thought he needed our help. And you can see, he's alone. He's got nobody." She pleaded with her eyes as best as she could, begging for understanding.

His fierce eyebrows relaxed a bit. His hands came off his hips and crossed over his chest. "Don't let it happen again. Tomorrow, we'll drive Jacob to the police station and leave him there. They'll find him a home."

"But…" The Look silenced her once again.

«»

Jan slept fitfully. How could Dad be so cruel? They had enough room, enough food. Couldn't he see what an asset the boy could be on the farm once he'd fattened up a bit? And it wasn't like people were taking in extra mouths to feed these days. Who knew where the boy would end up.

She awoke stiff and sore. After dragging herself out of bed, she dressed and got ready for breakfast. When she arrived in the kitchen, Mom was already putting food on the table.

Mom gave her a tired smile. "Knock on Jacob's door, please. Let him know breakfast will be ready soon."

Jan padded up the stairs and down the hallway to the spare bedroom. She knocked on the door. "Jacob, time for breakfast soon. You awake?"

No response.

Caleb met her in the hallway on his way to the kitchen.

She knocked again. "Jacob? You up?"

Still no response.

Caleb opened the door. The room was empty.

While they investigated, Dad poked his head into the room. "What's going on?"

Jan spoke first. "He's gone, Dad. We went to wake him up, but he's not here."

Dad didn't respond but strode to the kitchen, then into the laundry room. She and Caleb followed, and a shiver charged through her. The place where the vehicle keys hung was short by one set. Dad rushed outside with them close on his heels.

They were too late. Someone had stolen the truck.

Chapter Six

What an idiot she'd been. She should have seen Jacob was trying to scam her. Now it was too late. Breakfast had been a somber affair. Dad had been silent the entire meal, not making eye contact with her even once. She kept seeing Caleb steal glances at Dad. With his hardened face weighing on her, her stomach ached.

After breakfast, she helped Mom clear the table. As she washed the pans, Dad came up beside her and wrapped an arm around her shoulders. She froze in place, unable to make eye contact, her hands sinking in the soapy water. A tear slipped down her cheek, and she wiped it away with her sleeve.

He turned her to face him, then pulled her into tight a hug, ignoring her wet hands as they soaked the back of his shirt. "No sense crying over spilled milk, is there?"

At those words, she let out a full sob and cried into his chest like she hadn't done since she was five and the car ran over her kitten. Dad rubbed her back and let her cry it out.

After she'd calmed to the point of having hiccups—she hated the hiccups—he backed away and looked her in the eye. "It's light enough now to go out and look around. Let's make sure nothing else is missing."

Something else? Her shoulders drooped, but somehow, she

nodded and plunged her hands back into the sink.

"I'll finish up, sweetie." Mom edged her aside. "You go on with your dad and Caleb."

Grateful, Jan dried her hands the rest of the way.

The three of them moved to the laundry room to don their work boots. At the gun safe next to the washing machine, Dad entered the code and opened it.

"It's a new day." He handed a 9mm XD-M handgun with a holster to Caleb. "It's time to start preparations to protect ourselves and the farm."

Caleb accepted the weapon, unbuckled his belt, and slid on the holster loop, securing it in place.

Dad then pulled out a smaller 9mm Shield handgun with a holster and held it out to her. "I know you don't like guns. But I've taught you how to shoot and how to carry safely. You need to have it—just in case."

Her breakfast rose back up into her throat as she accepted the heavy weapon. Sure, her gun was lightweight compared to theirs, but it felt as if it carried the weight of the world. With trembling hands, she forced her belt through the holster loop and fumbled to secure the belt with the weight attached.

Dad secured a second 9mm XD-M to his belt. Then he removed a large rifle—the AR-15 that rarely saw daylight.

When they first moved to the farm, coyotes roamed in abundance. He'd taught her and Caleb how to shoot to protect the calves. He also ensured they knew gun safety. But that didn't make her comfortable with the sidearm weighing on her waistline.

They followed him back to the kitchen where he placed the enormous gun in the pantry, propped up against the front corner. Mom ignored the movement around her as she washed the pots. She didn't stop cleaning even when Dad came up beside her and slid an arm around her waist. Mom didn't like guns, so this might end in an argument.

Dad snugged Mom to his side. "It is only there for an emergency, luv. The safety is on."

She didn't respond.

Jan could barely breathe. The lump in her throat made it hard to swallow.

Dad waited for a few heartbeats, and then his lips flattened into a solid line, his eyes hardened. Removing his arm from around Mom, he beckoned Jan and her brother. "Well, let's go see what we find." He walked out the door and up the hill to the corral, the truck's parking spot. There, he inspected the ground. Near the end of the squeeze chute, the cows had trampled the grass into a muddy area during the health checks. He focused on it, staring at his own feet, then back at the muddy section, going back and forth. "Caleb, come over here."

When Caleb complied, Dad held up a hand to stop him just short of the area. "Stick your foot beside this print here in the mud, but don't push down."

Once again, Caleb complied.

Stooping, Dad traced a finger along something. "That's what I thought. It's too small to be my footprint but too big to be yours. And it is all over this area, next to Jacob's prints. He wasn't alone."

An icy chill crawled down Jan's back. Jacob had been working her all along.

How could I have been so stupid? He was a plant. He just wanted to steal from us, and I brought him right inside. Idiot!

She surged forward. "Dad, I—"

"Not now, Jan. I'm thinking."

Caleb glared at her. Right. No talking to Dad when he's working through a problem.

"Well, nothing to be done about this now, but we need to get better protection." He rubbed the back of his neck as he often did when thinking through a problem. "It's time to buy those dogs. Whatcha think, Caleb?"

A massive grin stretched out Caleb's face. "Definitely."

Jan almost rolled her eyes. He'd been wanting some German shepherds for years, eyeing flyers posted on the auction barn bulletin board. The man who raised dogs often showed up with trained animals to sell. They weren't cheap, but he guaranteed they were ready to protect.

Dad placed his hands on his hips and frowned at the long driveway. "The next question is—How are we going to get them home without a truck?"

Closing her eyes, Jan kneaded her forehead, a sudden throbbing there hurt like the kid had run the truck into it. That truck had been their lifeline. With it, they could buy and sell animals, take someone to the hospital, cart in supplies. They had planned on picking up a new bull for the second herd next month.

How could they now without a truck? They couldn't exactly walk a bull by hand for the thirty miles between the auction and home. Some farmers were still delivering, but they were fewer by the day as vehicles died. Spare parts, scarce as they were for repairs, pushed delivery costs sky-high.

That breakfast might come back up soon after all.

"Well, the golf cart could make the trip there. We may have to push it the last bit." Caleb swiped his brow with his sleeve. "But they have solar chargers to rev it back up for the return run."

With a big grin, Dad slapped Caleb's shoulder. "I like how you think. That'll be on the edge of the cart's range. In the meantime, let's figure out what we can afford to trade for the dogs while we check the perimeter."

They started toward the golf cart before Dad eyed her. "Want to come with us? Or would you prefer to go back to the house with your mom? You won't be going to the pea patch until we've checked for other intruders. Even then, you won't go there alone anymore."

"I'll go back and help Mom." She trudged back down the hill, kicking at loose stones along the way.

What a royal mess, and it was all her fault. Stupid.

«»

Mom had finished breakfast cleanup and sat on the couch mending another pair of jeans. When Jan slumped beside her, Mom nudged Jan's leg with her own. "You can take your gun off in the house."

"I don't want to wear it." Jan slouched against the canvas couch, the pallid cushions, so much like Mom, seeming to repel her with that atrocity on her hip. "It doesn't feel right. I can't shoot someone."

Mom worked the thread in a steady rhythm, not speaking until she lifted the pants to bite off the thread. "Done. Not a bad mending job, if I do say so myself." She held it between them, then patted Jan's knee. "Your father won't relent on this right now. So be careful with it and wear it outside until things calm down."

Jan wiggled around, trying to get the holster off her belt without getting up, but gave in and stood to remove it. She laid it on the end table and retook her seat.

"The minute you stand back up, the gun goes into the safe,

unless you're going back outside. Understood?"

Jan sighed, and her head drooped until her chin closed in on her chest. "Yes, ma'am." She leaned into Mom and rested her head on her shoulder, feeling five years old again. "I was such an idiot. I can't believe I let Jacob fool me and steal our truck. How are we going to survive if we can't buy and sell the cows?"

Mom tucked Jan under her arm and pulled them into a tight union. "It wasn't just you, sweetie. I trusted him too. He seemed so lost and neglected. Most likely, he is, and someone is manipulating him to steal."

"I'm going to throw up. Having to wear the guns—Dad and Caleb could get killed because of me."

Her mother shook her shoulder and, with her opposite hand, forced Jan's chin up to make eye contact. "Never say that again." A fierce mama-bear look bore down on her—Mom meant business.

"Yes, ma'am." As a single tear slipped down Jan's cheek, she swiped it away. "I'm going to go email Renee if I can get it to go through."

One last squeeze from her mom and Jan was up. As instructed, she stopped by the safe to secure the gun before going to her bedroom.

Once in her room, she plopped in front of an ancient laptop, a hand-me-down from her father. She remembered new laptops under the Christmas tree every year for one of them, even though the old ones still worked. Dad would always say, "You have to keep up with the technology. As soon as you buy a laptop, it's already out of date." Now they were fortunate to each have an old laptop that still worked. They had traded older ones to people who had none.

Computers were precious, even though they didn't work like

they used to. Parts were scarce for repairs if they broke, and the internet only functioned sporadically. The schools that had gone online at the startup of the new school year two years ago had given up entirely now. Even cell towers were inconsistent, so if a cell phone still worked, they used it more for texting than calling. Small devices were too difficult and expensive to replace. A person would have to be crazy to keep one in a pocket or backpack where it could get dropped or damaged.

She booted up the cranky machine and drafted a quick email.

Renee:

Rough day today. A kid tricked me into bringing him home, and he stole our truck. I'm such an idiot!

I miss you. I keep hoping your dad will decide to move back so we can see each other again. I can't trust anyone but you and my family now. Maybe your dad could bring you out to visit sometime?

Luv you,

Jan

She hit send. Somehow, the action felt so empty, as if she were sending a note out into the ocean in a bottle. Who knew if Renee would ever receive and read it? Her family had only one laptop, so if it broke, their connection to the world and Jan was gone. Renee wasn't often able to use the laptop because they babied it. Patience was the key, and Jan would have to wait for a response. Resting a hand against the clover-purple wall they'd had such fun painting, she ached from missing Renee and whispered a prayer for a reply.

《》

It was auction day. Right before bed last night, Jan overheard Caleb asking Dad whether he thought their golf cart had the full thirty-mile range it had when they bought it. Dad had merely said he hoped so.

Dad kept a calendar in the kitchen with all of the scheduled farm maintenance. The cart was on that list as well since proper maintenance was important if they wanted their equipment to last. She'd helped Caleb switch the batteries to the newest set to ensure a full charge.

With her gun strapped on and the smell of sun-warmed earth and grass surrounding her, she waited in the cart for Mom. Dad had already loaded up the back with a cooler full of one-pound packages of frozen ground beef to sell.

Caleb sat beside her in the middle seat, grinned, and gave her a shove. "Move over, Squirt. Big man in the seat needs room." When she shoved as hard as she could, then stuck her tongue out at him, he winked.

The door opened, and Mom stepped out. "I need an assist with my market box, please." Dad jogged back and reemerged with a crate piled high with canned and baked goods Mom had gathered. After Mom rested in the front seat and he'd stowed the goods in the back seat, it was time to be off.

Mom tapped Dad's shoulder. "One second, please." She turned back to Jan and Caleb. "A moment of prayer for a safe journey."

They all bowed their heads.

"Father, thank you for this beautiful day. The sunny skies are such a blessing. We ask that you get us the whole way to the auction and back safely. Please also help us make good sales and trades today and bless our efforts. Amen."

"Amen," Jan and Caleb chorused. Silence from Dad, though he was lifting his head at the end.

He shifted the cart into drive. "Let's go."

The thirty-minute trip took an hour and a half. The minute

Dad shifted the cart into park, Jan was up and out, grateful to stand after the long drive.

With the cart's limited space, the standard eight-foot sales table wouldn't fit, so a small card table had to suffice. After they unloaded the cart and set Mom's goods up on the table—blessedly in a shady spot—Dad positioned a folding stool behind the table and pointed it out to Mom. She rolled her eyes but sat.

He then surveyed the surrounding tables and auction barn. "Jan, stay with your mom today. No need to be wandering around by yourself."

Fine with her.

"Caleb, you and I are going to find those dogs. Perhaps we'll get someone willing to deliver that bull and maybe pick up a heifer or two next week for the sale."

While they headed off into the crowd, Jan sat in the grass beside her mom's stool. Mom tugged on Jan's ponytail and winked. "As long as you stay in eyesight, I'm sure you can go look around. I can handle the table."

"Thanks, Mom, but I'm good here."

"But market day is your favorite. I can smell boiled peanuts somewhere. Why don't you see if you can locate them?"

"I'm not hungry."

Mom jammed her hands on her hips. "You planning to be my permanent shadow?"

Jan glared right back.

On a typical market day, she'd be off the instant her mom opened for sales. One person could handle the traffic since so many people had tables to man. People worked in teams with one person wandering from table to table to make trades while the other manned their booth waiting. But Mom had nothing on her needs list today.

Since Renee had left, Jan would visit the other tables to talk and soak up stories of what was going on around the area. Word of mouth was the best source of information. Today, everyone seemed to scowl or have shifty-looking eyes. Was it her imagination? Or did they all look like they were up to no good?

She couldn't trust anyone. Mom needed protection since with her soft heart she'd never turn away anyone, especially if they appeared to be in need. Jan would have to move people along if they stayed and chatted too long. Friendships were a thing of the past. Guns and self-protection were the things of the present. She got it now. Better late than never.

«»

By the end of the day, she had collected every dandelion within fifty yards of their table and braided them into a wreath. The boredom of staying at the table drew the day out into an unbearably long stent. Mom's forehead glistened, even though the tree they'd set up near still provided shade from the afternoon sun.

Spotting Caleb and Dad returning, she jumped up from the ground and abandoned the wilting headdress. The quick step of the men's approach told her they were still in business mode.

"Found the dog handler." Caleb beamed. "We ordered two trained German shepherd guard dogs."

"The cost was steep, though." Dad rubbed his jaw, wincing a little as he made eye contact with Mom. "Two heifers."

Jan winced too as Mom closed her eyes and let out a shaky breath.

Caleb continued, unfazed. "The trainer will bring them to the farm tomorrow. The guy also agreed to deliver Dad's bull for the second herd."

"That isn't cheap either." Dad rested a hand over Mom's. "He wants a steer."

Jan pressed a hand to her stomach, queasy again. Three of this year's sale herd gone like the truck because of her mistake.

As Caleb and Jan packed up the cart with the remaining canned goods and the items Mom received in trade, Mom hugged Dad's arm to her. "Well, I've some good news. I had some people pay in silver coins today. Not too many, of course, but I'll take silver and gold anytime I can get it."

"That's good." Dad's shoulders stayed slumped. "Because I'll have to give up about a quarter of our remaining gold bars to get the bull."

"Wait till you see the dogs, though, Mom." Caleb jumped in. "They're amazing."

Some of the tightness loosened in Jan's tummy at seeing Caleb so animated about the dogs. Few things animated him enough to shed the stoic persona he'd adapted, but he'd wanted those dogs for a long time. She jammed some unsold canned peas into the back of the cart. Peas! She never wanted to see those wretched things again. It sure would be easier to enjoy Caleb's pleasure if her miserable mistake hadn't instigated the whole thing.

Dad had saved as much as he could to the purchase of the farm. Once the farm was theirs, he'd converted all his remaining assets into silver and gold, thinking they'd be the only currency to hold value if the economy collapsed. Not everyone accepted the precious metals anymore, but some still thought the economy would revive someday. If it did, then metals would have value paper never had. Not everyone could see past today, though, and food had more value than something that couldn't fill their bellies.

Caleb talked incessantly on the way home about the dogs, describing their size, their training, their eating and sleeping schedule, and their names, Max and Luna. On and on, he went. She wanted to be home to hide in her bedroom. If Caleb didn't stop talking about those dogs soon, she'd lose it.

«»

After breakfast, Caleb jumped up to help Mom clean the table without waiting for Jan to pitch in. Mom looked sideways at Dad and then back at Caleb's rushed pace. She remained seated, sipping her herb tea. As he wiped the last crumbs from the table, he paused. "I'm heading out to make a place for the dogs to bed down in the barn."

That explained it.

Dad cleared his throat. "You might need to help Jan get peas picked this morning first. The dogs won't be showing up for another hour. You've got time."

Caleb's head drooped. "Yes, sir."

Great. Now she had a babysitter—and an unhappy one. "I'll get my bucket and be ready in less than five." If she filled the bucket quickly, Caleb could be back before he resented her too much.

Still, she struggled to match his longer strides as they made their way to the garden. She had to take two steps for every one of his, and sweat broke out at the effort. With him oblivious to her plight, she felt too guilty to ask for mercy.

She was gulping for breaths while he opened the fence. He turned to get the bucket and winced. "Squirt, why didn't you say to slow down? I wasn't thinking."

"I'm... fine." Her gasps for air said otherwise.

"Take a break while I get started."

He didn't pick for long before she jumped in to assist. Caleb rarely talked when he was thinking about something he had to get done. He was so much like Dad. Feeling too guilty over him putting his morning plans on hold to babysit her, she didn't interrupt his thoughts.

They had filled the bucket before the sun reached the boiling stage, then headed back to the house at a more reasonable pace.

"Sorry, Caleb." She couldn't make eye contact.

She saw him look over at her in her peripheral vision.

"For what?"

"I know you hate having to come out here with me. I could have done this on my own." She kept her focus on her boots, kicking stones out of her way, not caring when she crushed vibrant clover blossoms.

"No way. We don't know who might wander onto our property these days. The dogs will take care of that, though."

His grin was back. And just like that, he'd forgotten his frustration. If only she could forget and forgive herself.

Back at the house, a large white dual-axle truck with a cattle trailer had parked before the house, and an older man stood in the carport with Dad. Two German shepherds sat behind the man, ears perked to attention. As soon as the dogs were in sight, Caleb let out a whoop and sprinted over to join the conversation. Jan trudged after him to meet the dogs.

Look at him. He's thrilled. I should be happy for him. Just wish they weren't guard dogs. My fault.

The man was explaining the training process. "I'll stay here for the evening, walking them around the perimeter fencing a few times. You'll need to accompany me to learn the commands."

It was going to be a long night. Dad and Caleb would work

with the dogs while she and Mom waited and prayed they'd be safe outside all night.

59

Chapter Seven

Mom joined her, staying up late talking and watching old DVDs, even consenting to binge Jan's favorite *Tomb Raider* movies. Jan snuggled in to the throw pillows while Mom brought over fresh-popped popcorn. Falling under the spell of U2's "Elevation," Jan gave in and sampled the tempting treat Mom offered. How long had it been since she'd had a girls' night? Good thing they had enough power in their solar batteries for the long night. Throughout the evening, either Dad or Caleb stopped by the house to get a drink, use the bathroom, or update them on how the dogs were doing. Running the entire perimeter of the one-hundred-acre farm enough times to make the trainer confident the dogs understood would take a while.

Exhausted after the sequel ended, Jan slumped and yawned. "I'm done. They can tell me all about it in the morning." She kissed her mom good night and went to bed. Though sleep overtook her as soon as her head hit the pillow, she woke often. She left the window open to hear any gunshots, all the while fearing the dogs would find someone and cause a confrontation.

When asleep, she dreamed of dogs chasing her. When awake, she swore she could hear them howling in a chase. In and out of sleep all night long, she suddenly startled awake. It was morning—barely. The sun was making the treetops visible in the orange skyline after the moonless night. Dad and Mom were murmuring in the kitchen below Jan.

After pulling on her jeans and a T-shirt, she padded downstairs to the kitchen, then slowed her approach. Had Mom looked so tired yesterday? With her eyes watery and red, she'd crossed her arms over her chest as if standing firm in a discussion.

"How do you know they're okay?"

Dad also had his arms crossed over his chest. "For the last time, they are fine. And it isn't our problem, anyway."

What happened? Had someone hurt the dogs?

"Is everything okay?" Jan asked.

They both turned, then relaxed their postures. Her parents never fought in front of them. Jan and Caleb had heard intense conversations behind closed doors before, but they were usually so muted the subjects of contention remained a mystery.

Dad walked over and drew her into a hug, then released her and tipped up her chin for eye contact. "Morning. Everything is fine."

While he poured himself another glass of water, Jan focused on her mom. "It sounded like something was wrong when you were talking."

Mom covered a yawn, then palmed dark hair away from her cheeks. "Max and Luna found something interesting on the path to the Boswells' place."

Interesting? Jan's heart gave a little start, and her eyebrows wrinkled as she stepped closer to Dad and gripped his arm. "What was it?"

He shifted his weight from one foot to the other. "It's not a problem. We sent the dogs to see what was up. Turns out we have new neighbors."

Butterflies took off in Jan's stomach. "Neighbors?"

"An RV parked in the Boswells' woods. We checked it out. A man and his teenage daughter are living in it. Your mom wanted to be sure they had enough food and a way to stay warm."

"That's right, sweetie. You know me. I'm always worried folks won't have what they need." Mom gathered her hair into a ponytail, then let it slip back over her neck before rubbing her hands together as if energized by a jolt of caffeine. "Let's get breakfast started."

Caleb tramped into the kitchen. "The dog handler left, and Max and Luna are eating their breakfast in the barn. He said they did well last night, so there was no need to stay any longer. He took the heifers."

"It's official, then." Dad slapped Caleb's back. "You are the proud owner of two guard dogs, son. You're in charge of taking care of them."

Caleb responded with a broad grin. "I'm starving. Let's eat."

«»

The next days stretched on in an eternity. Jan felt like a prisoner on the farm. Caleb accompanied her whenever she went pea picking. Some days, she went out with him and Dad to work on fences. Other days, she stayed in the house helping Mom process the peas or work in the greenhouse. Dad insisted she no longer work beyond the immediate vicinity of the house by herself. She missed her freedom to wander about the property.

Renee hadn't yet responded to the email. Perhaps her family's laptop had died on them. Maybe Jan would never hear from her best friend again. Maybe she no longer even had a best friend. Renee could be dead for all she knew.

What did it matter, anyway? Jan didn't need friends. She couldn't trust anyone. All that mattered was keeping her family safe.

Scowling, she contemplated her next chore—cleaning out the chicken coop. The little building stood in full view of the house, so she could work alone after cleaning up the lunch dishes.

She was putting away the last of the pans when Mom wandered into the kitchen. "Let's go on a field trip today."

Jan closed the cupboard door. "Field trip?"

"Let's go gather up some watercress from the creek." Mom smiled as if it were an everyday activity in their new reality.

"Um, we're not allowed off the property without Dad or Caleb. Remember?"

Mom winked. "Well, technically, the creek runs through the corner of our land. That makes it our creek, don't you think?"

Jan shook her head, her hands on her hips. "That's a long way to walk. I don't think it's a good idea." Today would be a hot one. The last thing she needed was for Mom to get too far away from the house in the heat of the day.

"I've walked that path a thousand times, and you know it." Mom pulled a basket out of the pantry and a few tea towels. "Now either you come along, or I go by myself. Your call."

"Dad's going to be mad." Jan snapped the words, hoping to get Mom's attention. Why did Mom have to be so stubborn? Perhaps she could talk Mom out of the crazy move.

"He'll be happy to have greens while we wait for the last batch of lettuce." Mom then moved toward the door and put on the boots from the rack. "Coming?" She stepped outside and headed toward the creek.

If Jan didn't go, Dad would be even angrier with her for letting Mom go alone.

"Hold up." Jan hurried to the door, first grabbing the hated gun out of the safe. She had to run to catch up to her mother, who was humming a tune Jan didn't know.

Getting to the creek took a while. Fortunately, the day wasn't to the scorching stage yet and low humidity. With the sun shining above and the birds singing, it was a gorgeous day for a walk. Savoring the flowers growing wild in the field, she forgot the weight on her belt. She picked a few red clovers as they walked, one of the prettiest of the spring field flowers. The cows loved them, so they'd disappear quickly after the men moved the herd into this pasture.

At the edge of the woods, they followed the fence line to the creek, then opened the nearby gate and headed into the woods. The creek ran clear today since it hadn't rained in a while. Watercress grew lush on its edges.

It was easy to get absorbed in the creek while picking watercress. She let her fingers swirl in the small eddies created by the flowing stream. Frolicking frogs, lizards, and salamanders added to the pleasure of the adventure, making her forget she was here to pick the peppery-tasting plant. Best to pick the young leaves as the older ones could be bitter.

Jan listened to Mom's humming as she plucked the greenery and placed it on the dampened tea towels. Jan helped, doing her best to leave the roots intact for future harvests. Soon, Mom pulled her boots off and waded into the current barefoot. Clearing her throat as she stared at Jan, Mom wiggled her toes in the water, then grinned and winked.

Jan let out a laugh. They'd done this since she was little. She tugged off her boots and waded in front of her mom—

toe wrestling. Mom couldn't beat Jan every time like she did when she was little. They were soon giggling like elementary students at recess.

Then a throat cleared behind them.

They jumped, screeching.

A man stood there with a girl about Jan's age. He held a bucket with watercress sticking out of the top. "Sorry, didn't mean to scare you. I'm your new neighbor, Daniel Tilbrook. And this is my daughter, Lizzy."

Jan scrambled to help Mom out of the water and grab their boots.

Mom gave him a nervous smile while she fought to get the second boot on over her wet foot. It finally slid on.

Jan shoved both her boots on, and her pant legs knotted up, half in and half out of the uncomfortable wet footwear.

"Nice to meet you, Daniel. I'm Marie Worthington, and this is my daughter, Jan." Mom nodded toward her. "Neighbors, huh? Did you buy the property next door? I hadn't seen a for-sale sign. They had locked the house up tight when they left."

Mr. Tilbrook put his arm around his daughter. "Not so permanent. We've been wandering a bit since we lost Lizzy's mom last year to the variant. We're taking a break from moving around since we saw the unoccupied home. Haven't gone into the house, though." His eyes tightened slightly. "We're not thieves."

He eyed Jan's hip—her holstered gun.

She'd forgotten she was wearing it. A lot of good it did her if she couldn't remember she had it when trouble came.

"The former occupants are friends of ours," Mom said. "They moved to the city to find work. We promised to watch their property for them." She moved a step closer to Jan as she spoke. "As long as you do no harm and leave the house alone, I don't think they'd mind sharing the property for a few days."

The hard line of Mr. Tilbrook's mouth softened, and then the edges of his lips curved up. "It's good to have neighbors who care for each other. I hope we can show ourselves as the sort you'll be happy to have next door. Best be going, Lizzy. We don't want our watercress to wilt before we get back home."

"If I may suggest"—Mom gestured to her basket—"it helps to keep a dampened cloth in the basket while you're picking. Prevents wilting."

"Well, thanks for that. It was nice to have met you. If you ever need anything, you know where we're at." They both walked away.

Once they were out of sight, Mom slipped an arm around Jan's waist. "That was a bit of a fright, at least for me."

"I'll say. I can't believe they were all the way back here at the creek. Scared the silly out of me."

Mom scooped up the basket she'd put down for the toe-wrestling match. "Let's get back home. Probably best not to mention our brief foray to the creek to your father. We'll just give this watercress to the cows. I'm sure they'll enjoy it."

Jan wouldn't have argued for any reason. "Amen, Mom. Amen."

«»

With the workdays full of more tasks than time to check them off, it was already time to head back to the auction. Jan had been canning peas and had a dozen jars to take. Mom had cut some old clothes too worn out to repair into squares. Though she didn't want to quilt, some women in town did and would trade for the material swatches.

After stowing the crate with jars and materials, Jan settled into the golf cart. Caleb came out with a box and joined her. She peeked into the box at his carved salad bowl with wooden serving spoons. "Nice job, Caleb. Does Mom know you're taking those to sell?"

"She said if I sell these, I have to make her a set next time. I've got an entire pin oak tree we had to cut down in the north pasture. It's not like I'll run out of wood soon. I'm asking a lot, though. It took forever to make the spoons right."

Mom and Dad settled in their seats. Before heading out, Dad checked for the third time. "Everyone got what they need? I'm not turning back once I head down the driveway."

"Yes," they chorused. Dad was a man on a mission today. At breakfast, he'd talked about negotiating a reasonable price for five heifers they were ready to sell. They needed a bull at a good price. Otherwise, the second herd wouldn't happen this year.

Because they didn't have a truck, they couldn't bring the heifers to the auction with them. Dad would have to find farmers who had already purchased from him and knew his stock. Sight unseen was a hard sell. People believed in each other in the country, but trust only went so far since those cattle represented serious money.

Max and Luna were off hunting the well-worn path circling the farm. They seemed to enjoy their runs and had goofy dog grins each time they returned. Knowing the dogs would protect the farm in their absence reassured her. She'd already cost the family enough.

After a long but uneventful drive, they unpacked and set up their wares. With Caleb sticking by the table to talk to potential customers who wanted to order from him, it felt crowded.

Jan hopped up and brushed off the seat of her jeans, nothing bothering to smooth down her market-day T-shirt—purple with some butterflies Mom embroidered for her birthday. "I'm going to wait in the cart."

Mom squinted at her. "For two hours? Why don't you go look around if you don't want to hang with us?"

"Am I allowed to this time?" Dad hadn't expressly forbidden her from going anywhere. Perhaps the rules were relaxing.

"Just check back in every half hour, okay? Go make a friend."

Like that was going to happen. Hadn't Mom learned anything from their mistake?

Jan wandered from table to table, standing far enough back that the owners wouldn't engage her in conversation. There were some interesting wares for sale. People were getting more experienced in creating alternatives for items that used to be cheap commodities. With wheat flour scarce, someone offered acorn flour and handwritten recipe cards to make bread. She'd have to tell Mom about that one.

Another table had baby rabbits hopping about in a pen underneath. Investigating their enclosure were black, brown, white, and mixed-colored bunnies with adorable ears and twitchy pink noses. Sure, the rabbits' destinies most likely involved stew pots, but perhaps Dad would let her keep one or two as pets. As soon as the table owner was engaged in negotiations with a potential buyer, Jan kneeled and petted a brown bunny's velvety fur. She could have rubbed the little animal for hours. Connecting to an innocent life felt so relaxing.

"Hi there." A girl popped down beside her, too close for comfort.

Jan jumped back up and hit her head against the table. "Sugarplum fairies!" She rubbed her sore skull.

The girl stood up. "Sorry, didn't mean to startle you—we

met out by the creek, remember—I'm Lizzy, and you're Jan, right? I wanted to say hi again when I saw you." The words came out in rapid-fire like one long run-on sentence.

Ah, yes—Lizzy. The rail-thin girl had tucked her curly brown hair into a baseball cap, and the ponytail bounced as it hung out the back. She jammed her hands into the pockets of her clean but well-worn jeans and scuffled old boots before latching onto Jan with hungry eyes.

A quick lurch jolted Jan's heart like someone was trying to jump-start it. But she jerked back a step and hardened her jaw. She wasn't interested in being friendly or making any friends. "I remember. I've got to get back to my mom's table." She started back at a brisk pace.

Lizzy followed, quick-stepping to keep up. More words spilled out as if she had diarrhea of the mouth. "Thought we could be friends since we're neighbors, you know. I don't know anyone around here. And Dad's got to go find work, so maybe I can come to your place sometimes during the day?"

In her peripheral view, Jan could see Lizzy's freckles and the girl trying to smile between words like she was doing her best to come across as friendly.

You won't fool me so easily. I know how this works now.

"No, I can't. I'm not allowed to have friends." Ouch. What a rotten lie. Jan never had been quick with excuses or fibs, but surely, the girl would give up and go away.

"That's the silliest thing I ever heard." Lizzy flicked her ponytail away from her face. "You're making it up."

Persistent thing. Jan nearly snorted. She'd give her that much. She picked up the pace even more and zigzagged through the tables to shake the girl.

Soon, Lizzy fell behind, and her parting words sounded a few yards behind her. "Okay then. I'll talk to you later. See ya."

And then Jan was alone again. Alone wasn't fun, but it was necessary. Strangers brought trouble and risk. She had to protect her family.

She circled the area to ensure Lizzy wasn't following her, going in and out of the auction buildings and around sellers' tables. Once sure she'd lost her, Jan doubled back and met up with Mom and Caleb.

Mom was finishing up with a customer, but Caleb watched her approach. "Can you watch my stuff? If anyone asks, Mom already knows the pitch."

Glad for the excuse to stay at the table, Jan nodded.

"Find anything interesting?" Mom nudged her with a shoulder. "Meet anyone new?"

She didn't want to broach the subject of Lizzy. "Acorn flour. We should try it. Don't you think?"

"Sure." Mom's eyes wrinkled in question. "And did you meet anyone new?"

"Saw tons of people. Most of them have been here before, though. You know, the usuals." Could she avoid the subject long enough to get out of admitting she'd seen Lizzy? "Look, Dad's coming back. Maybe he sold the heifers."

Saved by her father's arrival. But the news wasn't good. The day had been a bust for Dad.

"I couldn't sell those heifers for anything." Dad pulled out a handkerchief to wipe his sweaty forehead, then ran it along the back of his neck. "My usual customers aren't here today. I couldn't find anyone willing to come out to the farm to inspect the cattle, either. They can't waste the gas and will wait until I can get the steers to the auction."

If they couldn't sell the steers, there would be no purchase of a bull.

"And without that extra income, I'm not willing to part with much of the gold we have right now. The new herd will have to wait," Dad finished.

Mom wasn't one to let the bad news linger. She rubbed his arm and wobbled up a smile. "No sense worrying about it anymore today. Let's just pray for a solution. Shall we?"

After Caleb returned, they packed up and headed home. During the long drive, Dad was silent while Mom chattered about seeds she'd plant in the garden since the peas were no longer producing. With plans to start in the greenhouse and to sow directly outdoors, there'd be plenty of gardening for the whole family this week.

«»

Weeks of long days and hard work passed. A no-till garden had been one of Mom's initial goals, and reducing the need for a gas-powered tiller had taken prominence with fuel in short supply. Although preparing the soil, planting, and then weeding the garden were all manual tasks, having enough produce to eat, preserve, and sell required an enormous garden.

Each night, Jan returned to the house covered in red clay and composted manure. The tough days left her soaked with sweat and smelling like she could fertilize the garden with her stained clothing.

Tonight, she was luxuriating in a cool shower. Usually, a hot bath was her favorite, but after getting so overheated today, even the thought of more warmth left her dizzy. After stripping off her icky clothing, she slid into the shower and put her head under the cool spray. Heaven on earth. Closing her eyes, she thanked God again for their deep well. With such a large reservoir, they'd never run it dry, and she could indulge in long, guilt-free showers.

After heat no longer radiated from her core, she got out and wrapped her body in a fluffy pink bathrobe—a Christmas present from Caleb last year. Yes, he'd found it at the auction, used, but it was still fluffy and pink.

She padded back to her bedroom and pulled out some clean clothes for supper when she heard shouting, barking, and yelping in the kitchen below. After dressing, she hurried down.

Blood spattered the wood floor, Caleb, and one of the German shepherds beside him. Max was whining as Caleb and Mom spoke to him in soothing tones. Crouched on the floor, Mom was trying to inspect his leg, and whenever she touched on painful areas, the dog yipped. Luna was dancing around the outside circle of her partner and the family, trying to nose in closer to her friend.

Jan hurried over. "How can I help?"

Mom looked up, her brow furrowed. All business. "Grab some bandages from the first aid kit. I think he needs stitches, but it's hard to tell for sure."

Caleb stroked Max's back and murmured soothing words. "It's okay, buddy. You're going to be fine."

Jan ran to the bathroom for the first aid kit, then opened the box and handed the bandages over. "Want some antibiotic ointment?"

"No." Mom shook her head. "We need to get the bleeding under control and get him to Doc. Run out and find Dad. He was going to the orchard to check on the fruit. Ring the bell on the front porch. If he can hear it, he'll head our way. Then get to the orchard."

"Yes, ma'am."

Jan sprinted to the porch, grabbed the striker for the triangle bell, and smacked it as loud and fast as she could. Next, she ran back into the house for her sneakers—no clunky steel-toed boots for sprinting. She threw them on and tied them sloppy but tight. She ran full speed toward the orchard.

Less than five hundred yards away, she developed a stitch in her side and had to catch her breath. Bent over, sucking in gasps of air, she heard a beautiful sound—the quiet hum of the golf cart heading her way.

Dad stopped the cart beside her. "Get in. What's wrong?"

He didn't wait for her to explain. Instead, he hit the accelerator as soon as she sat.

"Max—hurt—bleeding. Doc."

"Got it."

Six small words were all they needed as she struggled to slow her breathing. Back at the house, she sprinted behind him as he charged inside.

Caleb still sat on the floor—more of Max's blood on the front of his shirt. He stroked the dog's head, who seemed calm. A swath of bandages covered Max's leg, and Luna lay nearby with Mom petting and comforting her.

As they entered, Caleb let out a heavy breath. "Looks like he needs stitches, Dad."

"Let's get him loaded. We should still have enough charge to get him there."

Caleb picked Max up, which caused a fresh yip followed by whining. Luna jumped up to follow.

"I don't think so, girl." Dad caught her by the collar. "Jan, keep hold of Luna."

Jan wrapped her hand around Luna's collar, straining to keep the dog inside while Caleb carried Max out the door.

The afternoon crawled by. Dusk was settling in when the golf cart trundled back down the driveway and into the carport.

She jumped off the chair, tossing her book on the side table. Would Max be okay?

Luna had paced for a full hour after they left before settling down by the door. The dog stood, barking to be let out to find her friend. She'd heard the cart before Mom or Jan and jumped at the door, frantic. When Jan opened it, Luna dashed out to greet Max.

Caleb carried Max inside with Luna prancing around them. Jan ground her teeth until Max struggled to get down, showing spunk again. Caleb lowered Max to the floor, and the two dogs came together, touching noses, then sniffing each other. Luna then spent a significant amount of time thoroughly inspecting and smelling Max's bandaged leg.

"Doc said he'll be good as new in a couple of weeks, but he's not allowed to patrol until those stitches heal." Caleb scrubbed a hand over his face. His dark hair stuck up at odd angles as if he'd been tugging at it. "I guess they're house dogs for now. You're sleeping with me, Max."

Max looked up at his master at the sound of his name, tail beating a quick rhythm. Not to be ignored, Luna plopped down into a perfect sit pose, ears perked for instructions, tail still in anticipation.

"Yes, Luna. I see you. You can come too."

She jumped up and ran in circles around Max and Caleb as if she understood.

Jan had to laugh. "Come here, Luna. You're going to trample your brother, and he needs to rest."

Luna bounded and accepted head scratches.

Jan spread her fingers through the wiry fur, warmth filling her as she related to the dog who'd been so worried about her brother—just like Jan had been after Caleb's injury earlier this spring. Then her fingers stilled, and she tipped her head to Caleb. "What happened to Max? Did Doc know?"

"He couldn't be positive." Caleb was tugging at his hair again. Poor guy. "But he thought a wild pig had tangled with him."

No way. "Since when do we have wild pigs?"

"Apparently, since today," Dad said. "Now, we don't have any dogs to deter them. That means it's pig-hunting season."

After smoothing his hair back into place, Caleb nodded his agreement.

Chapter Eight

"Mom, I haven't heard from Renee in months." Jan stood at the counter, peeling eggs, while Mom sat at the kitchen bar. Dad and Caleb were out hunting for pigs. "I'm worried something has happened to her."

Mom's fingers stilled over the embroidery work in her lap. "Did you try to email her father as well? Perhaps she's just been busy."

Jan rinsed the last egg under the faucet. After the remaining bits of shell washed into the sink, she placed the egg into the bowl for storage. "I didn't think to try that. I'll go send him a note."

She trotted up the stairs to her bedroom, unearthed the old laptop, and booted it up. It ran so slow these days, she had plenty of time to change into her pajamas for the evening while she waited. Comfortable in her nightclothes, she pulled the computer over to her bed and placed a book between her lap and the machine. Then her fingers typed faster than the old machine could keep up with.

Mr. Boswell:

I hope you are doing well. My family is fine, though we miss seeing you and yours. I've been trying to reach Renee for a while now, but she hasn't responded. If you read this message, could you ask her to respond to me? I want to know she's okay. If she's sick or something, please let me know! I'm worried.

Jan

She'd never emailed Renee's dad before, but Dad used to correspond with him about the cows.

He's got to be there. I need someone to connect with besides my family. I miss her so much.

Nothing to do but wait now. She flopped back on her duvet, the string of light-up butterflies above her swaying like living things in the air conditioning breeze. Drawing in a slow breath, she focused on their gossamer wings, vivid against the clover walls. Renee helped her decorate a lifetime ago, back when their biggest worry was whether the home team was going to win Friday night's game. Renee *had* to be all right.

With a groan, Jan slammed her arm over her eyes and just laid there. With the internet connection so poor, it made little sense to try to do anything else. The computer would most likely be attempting to transfer the email out for hours before it succeeded.

Man, she missed her music—and Photoshop. She needed inspiration right now—a best friend chattering at her side, delightful music streaming through her earbuds, a fast laptop balancing on her knees, and a magical world unfolding through her art program.

Her fingers twitched to create something. She'd never been great at drawing, but with those old art programs, she'd been able to express herself in enchanted designs. Her art teachers had praised her, and her guidance counselor had said she'd thrive in an advertising career. She'd thought she had life all planned out.

Now, what lay ahead?

<«»>

Weeding, weeding, and more weeding. Jan and Caleb spent each morning in the garden pulling up young weeds before the shoots had the chance to become unmovable in the red Georgia clay. They started early to avoid noon's intolerable heat.

Jan paused from her work and leaned on her hoe. "Caleb, do you ever wonder what happened to all of our friends?"

Grunting as he uprooted a giant pokeweed, he responded. "We know what happened, Squirt. They all moved into Columbus or up to Atlanta to find work or help."

"No, I mean, I haven't heard from Renee in months. For all I know, her whole family caught the variant and died. We don't *know*, do we? They may never come back. Then what?" She rested her head on her arms, standing in the middle of her cornrow.

Caleb paused and rubbed the pokeweed sprout between his fingers, frowning at the red-dirt stains. "Why be a Negative Nellie? Someday, we'll see everyone again." He tossed the weed aside and stooped to pluck another. "Unless you get skinned alive for not doing your share of the weeding, that is."

She snatched up a clump of weeds with a huge clod of dirt still attached and threw it at him, hitting him squarely in the back—then ran as fast as her feet would carry her toward the house.

His footfalls grew louder as he caught up outside the garden. A look back revealed a clump of dirt and weeds in his hands. "You're in trouble now, Squirt." He snagged her shirt from behind and held the weapon above his head.

Squeals of laughter erupted. "No—I give—"

Laughing, Caleb pulled her shirt away from her sweat-drenched back and thrust the clod up the shirt, then rubbed it into her bare skin. Squirming as he created a muddy mess, she lost her balance, and he fell with her into a heap of giggles and guffaws.

A dirt and grass fight ensued. First Caleb and then she each crawled around, picking up hunks of grass and dirt they'd pitched out of the garden earlier. Clods of earth flew as they tried to deposit dirt into each other's clothing. Soon, exhausted, they rolled apart to recover.

Jan shook her shirt out and tried to shake out her pant legs. Clumps plopped onto her boots. She'd have dirt in all her cracks and crevasses for the rest of the day. But goofing around had been fun.

A shiver traced the length of her spine as she rested her hands on her knees and eyed him. "It may be just you and me taking care of each other when we're adults. Did you ever think of that?"

He swiped the back of his arm across his forehead, leaving a muddy streak, then got back on his feet, and put his hand out to help her up. "Nope. Not gonna happen. I'm going to find myself a beautiful woman to marry." He winked. "Then I'll consider taking care of your skinny butt later."

She twisted her lips into a wry smile. "Ha ha."

Walking back to their hoes and rows, Caleb brushed dirt off himself. Good. He was also trying to shake dirt out of his pant legs. She gave as good as she got. She smirked. Served him right.

Whoa. She stilled as Luna and Max barked at some perceived threat. Intermingled with the barking came a female shouting. "No! Bad! Go away!"

Without bothering to discuss the issue, they sprinted toward the sounds.

She couldn't keep up with Caleb's top speed, but she did her best to stay within in eyesight as he charged toward the commotion. They made it to the perimeter path and through a cluster of pine trees, then out into a field. At the field's edge, the dogs had cornered a girl against an oak tree.

As Caleb approached, he slowed. "Off!"

Max and Luna stopped barking and backed away but continued to pace in front of her.

Oh no. That Lizzy just won't go away, will she?

Caleb reached the dogs and stopped, bending at his waist and gulping in air. "Sit."

Max and Luna sat, ears perked, not five feet away from Lizzy.

Serves her right. What's she doing on our land, anyway?

Jan joined Caleb in gulping down air. She really needed to get more cardio in.

"Hi, Jan," Lizzy said. "I'll bet you are wondering what I'm doing here, huh? Long time no see. Those are some guard dogs. I didn't see them until they were practically on top of me. Who'd have thought they could sneak up on a person and be so loud once they caught up?"

More diarrhea of the mouth. Ugh.

Jan's glaring eye contact silenced Lizzy.

Eyeing Jan, Caleb raised his eyebrows.

How do I explain I've met Lizzy without explaining the watercress incident? Maybe he won't ask.

"Caleb, you've met Lizzy." Breathe out. "Our temporary neighbors." Breathe in. "Squatting on Boswell property." Even with the extra breaths, Jan still managed some derision. "Lizzy also likes to stalk people on auction day."

Having caught his breath, he folded his arms across his chest, his best football linemen pose. "Hey, Lizzy. Whatcha doing on our land?"

A huge smile crinkled up her freckled face. "Oh, that—I was picking watercress in the creek. The creek on the other side of the fence isn't yours too, is it? Anyway, saw some mushrooms here in the field—thought they'd go well with the watercress. Dad couldn't come with me today—looking for work—thought I'd surprise him."

Man, bouncing from foot to foot, the girl practically vibrated with pent-up energy.

One of Caleb's eyebrows rose more significantly. "Mushrooms? I don't think anything growing out here right now is edible. Do you know what's safe to eat?"

Her glow extinguished. "Oh."

Jan twitched her own eyebrows.

Who'd have thought Lizzy was capable of a single-syllable response?

Caleb walked over and lifted the bucket Lizzy still had clutched by the handle. "If I were you, I'd pitch those mushrooms. And you might want to pitch the watercress and start again since you seem to have gotten mushroom pieces throughout the greens."

A pout pushed out Lizzy's lips as he let go, and she upended the bucket, dropping its contents on the ground.

Jan harrumphed.

More silence? May need to look for pigs flying nearby.

"If you cross over the fence, then you are on our land," Jan said. "And how'd you get over it, anyway? It should have shocked the dickens out of you."

"Really? I just crawled between the two wires. I didn't think it could be on. You folks have electric?" She was bouncing again. "That's so awesome! In your house too? Can I come check it out? What else do you have? Wait till I tell Dad! He's going to want to come see. Do you have electric *all* the time?"

"Whoa, slow down there," Caleb said. "Do you ever take a breath?"

Lizzy clamped her mouth shut.

Caleb forked his fingers through his dark hair, frowning at the fence line. "We need to figure out where the fence broke. And you need to head back home, Lizzy. Nice to see you, again." He walked toward home. "Come."

As the dogs followed their master, Jan started to follow as well, but then paused. "You need to keep off our land. As you can see, we have guard dogs. I wouldn't want anything to happen because of your trespassing." After giving the last word plenty of emphasis, she hurried to catch up with her brother and retrieve their tools.

From behind them came one last spout. "Bye then—nice to meet you, Caleb—see you at the auction tomorrow?"

The girl just wouldn't give up, would she?

They both ignored her.

«»

They'd loaded up their wares and tucked the card table in the golf cart's third-row seat. It would be another long ride to the auction.

"You're sure cranky." Caleb nudged her.

Every time they puttered to the auction in the golf cart, the guilt of losing the truck charged back with far more power than the pitiful cart could muster.

She crossed her arms over her chest. "And you seem excited. Are you expecting to see something interesting? Or perhaps *someone* interesting?"

The last time, Caleb spent a particularly long time explaining the virtues of his whittled salad bowls to a blond girl about his age. She'd been pretty for sure. Caleb had been excruciatingly cheerful all the way home that day.

"Who knows? The auction always has something interesting to see." He bumped his shoulder against hers.

Once they'd set up, Mom asked her to see if she could find the acorn flour again. It wasn't Jan's favorite since it didn't rise like wheat flour, but if they mixed wheat and acorn, it was tolerable. She dreaded the day when the wheat flour ran out.

Jan headed toward the far end of the auction grounds. The acorn flour vendor was usually on the opposite side from where Mom set her table up. With Dad less concerned about security lately, Jan could wander around again.

The bunny vendor was hard to pass by. She wanted to pet the furry babies, but Lizzy surprised her there last time. She couldn't risk a repeat.

Come to think of it, I should stay around the edges of the auction so I can see her coming before she sees me.

Jan made a beeline for the edge of the crowd, then found the vendor. The woman who worked at the table was busy with another customer.

"No, my prices are fair." The trader told a young woman with a toddler on her hip. "I'm not a charity here. I need to eat too."

"I guess the kids will be without bread this week then." A grimace twisted the young woman's face as she stormed away.

Man, negotiations could be tough. Some vendors were less flexible than others. Best to start out positive, though.

"Morning." Jan smiled as if it were the best morning ever. "I'd like to trade for some of your flour. What's your asking price today?"

"You have more of those canned peas? Those were the best I've had in years."

"I need a five-pound bag of flour. I can offer you a half-dozen jars of those peas."

"That's only about one jar per pound." The woman's lips formed into a thin line, and her eyebrows knit together. "Do you know how much work goes into one pound? You need to make that two dozen."

"Do you know how many pea pods I have to pick in the heat to make one jar of peas?" *Play it up good. You only get one shot at this.* "But I'll make you a deal. I'll give you two jars per pound. That means ten jars for five pounds." *Bring it home now—use those advertising skills you once thought would bring you a bright future.* "And that's a bargain."

As the woman paused, Jan held her breath. There weren't that many jars left if she'd just bartered away almost a dozen of her hard-earned jars.

"Okay, deal." The woman held out her hand to shake. "But be back here in no less than a half hour. I've got to sell all of this today, and I'm not holding your bag out from sale if someone else has their trade with them."

Jan nodded, then jogged back toward Mom's table.

Once again, she skirted the crowd, but this time, she went the opposite way to see if she could find anything new and interesting. As she neared the halfway point back to their table, a child stood on the edge of a wooded area by the road. The child had a blanket over its head, so Jan couldn't see if it was a boy or a girl.

As she drew closer, she frowned at the child's filthy blanket and the small hands, dark brown with dirt, holding it tight. No shoes covered the once-white socks—at least the top layer of sock looked white. It appeared the child wore multiple layers of socks.

"Do you have any food?" When the child looked up at her, she froze, and a fizzle zinged down her back—Jacob!

The boy skittered a step sideways, and breath hissed from his lungs. "Jan?"

He froze, then sprinted into the woods. A momentary shock paralyzed her before she took off after him. "Jacob, stop. Come back here."

How could he run so fast in just socks?

The front of the woods was mature oak trees, but a few yards beyond those was nothing but scrub. The area had obviously been clear-cut about five years ago of the Georgia pine. The owners hadn't replanted, so a mess of scrub trees and old stumps now tangled with the undergrowth. It was like running an obstacle course blind, and Jacob had blended right in. It was no use.

"Jacob!" she screamed. "You get back here. That truck isn't yours. I'm going to find you."

She stopped and listened. But the woods betrayed no movement, only the sound of small animals and her own heavy breathing.

Wait until Dad hears Jacob is still in the area.

The truck might be around here too. This wasn't over yet.

Chapter Nine

She hustled back to the family's table, out of breath by the time she reached it. Leaning over, she braced both hands on her thighs and pushed out words between gulps of air. "Mom—Jacob here. We have to—police. Maybe they—find truck."   It jumbled out in a rush before Jan straightened her hunched stance.

"Whoa, slow down. Where's Jacob?" Mom put a hand on Jan's shoulder as if to weigh her down to earth.

Jan took a deep breath and slowed her speech, waving one hand toward the woods. "He went in there. I lost him in the scrub. Maybe Dad and Caleb could find him." She clenched her fist, desperate to repair her mistake.

"If he's in the brush, we'd best leave it to the police." Mom rubbed Jan's shoulder. "It's too easy for him to hide in that mess."

Jan wanted to cry. To have him so close and have lost him—it was another huge mistake. They needed the truck. She needed life to go back to normal.

"I can go look again, around the edges. He was looking for food. Hunger might make him try to find another person to trick."

And I'll be waiting for him this time.

Mom turned her so they were eye to eye. "No, sweetie. You don't need to find him right now. He has an adult with him, remember? You don't want to run into a strange man in that scrub. Right?"

She'd forgotten about that.

Shoot.

Jan dropped her head in defeat.

"How'd your bargaining go? Did you reach a deal on the flour?" Mom's voice was bright, as if nothing bad had happened. How could she be so cheerful when disaster had struck again?

"I just need to take some peas over. The trade is good." Resigned, Jan collected her jars into a small wooden box while Mom gave her shoulder one last comforting rub and moved to talk to a new customer.

Jan trudged back to the acorn vendor, looking at every child's face as she passed. That dirty blanket was probably to make him look cold and forlorn so people would take pity on him—the snake in the grass.

Plenty of people were at the auction today, and she didn't see any sign of Jacob's dirty little hands and feet again. Dad was at the table with Mom when Jan brought back the acorn flour and empty jars from the trade.

"So, you saw Jacob again, huh?" Dad dropped an arm around her and jostled her. "Let's go talk to the police. There's an officer stationed in the auction barn."

«»

The police weren't helpful. At least not from her point of view. Just told Dad there wasn't much they could do and apologized. The officer hadn't even taken out a notebook to write a report. He just leaned against his patrol car in the parking lot.

Jan elbowed forward. "But you have to go search the woods," she protested. "He's still in there. I'm sure of it."

There had to be a way to motivate this guy.

Dad grasped her arm and squeezed. Nodding at the officer, he said, "I'm sure the officer knows what he can and can't do, Jan."

She scowled at the ground. Jacob was just getting away with it—again. *I'll tie his little butt to a tree the next time I see that conniving thief.*

"Little lady," the officer drawled, "I know it's frustrating, but we don't have the manpower or the resources to go hunting for a child in a thicket."

She gritted her teeth against his relaxed posture and condescending smile. Little lady? She wasn't a child.

Elbows against the car hood, he squinted at the sun as if judging the remaining daylight. "I have more pressing issues, such as keeping people safe and alive. Theft is pretty low on the priority list these days."

Dad must have seen her frustration because he once again squeezed her arm as if in a warning to behave.

"Yes, sir," she muttered.

"Now, if you know for sure where the stolen truck is located, we could check it out for you." The officer addressed Dad. "Other than that, we can't use gasoline to search willy-nilly."

"Thank you for your time, officer." Dad gave a nod. "We'll let you know if we have any such information." He tugged at her sleeve. "Let's head back to your mom, kiddo. I'm sure she's getting ready to pack up for the day."

Kiddo. Little lady. Willy-nilly. She ground her teeth beneath her polite smile, then dragged her feet back to their sales table where Mom and Caleb had already packed everything up.

"Anything they can do?" Mom asked. Hopeful eyes scanned their faces.

Jan couldn't maintain eye contact with her. Dad's reaction to the officer had been frustratingly calm. If it had been up to her, they would've demanded more help. The truck had been their lifeline.

"We're on our own," Dad said. "But I doubt the vehicle is still around, anyway. And I doubt you'll see that boy again soon either, Jan."

He gathered Mom into a hug. "We'll figure it out. We always do, right?"

"We always do," Mom responded. "Let's head home."

«»

It was her favorite time of the year—calving season. Twice each day, they checked on all the pregnant cows to ensure all was well. All those adorable baby calves would run around, jumping and playing before long. This morning, she tagged along with Caleb on the first run.

As they passed through the far northeast pasture, one cow was standing by herself on the opposite side of the field from where the herd grazed. Something was up. By the time they came alongside her, she was making strange huffing and coughing sounds. When Caleb drove up, she walked away but paused after a few feet.

"What's wrong, mama?" He spoke in a soothing tone, getting out of the cart and approaching from the rear.

"Is she okay?" Jan hadn't heard these sorts of sounds out of a cow before. Was it sick?

"She's in labor. Looks like it's been a while, though. She may not be able to get the baby out. We need to bring Dad." He let out a long hard breath, then clucked his tongue. "He may have to pull the calf."

Jan suppressed a shiver. She hadn't yet seen a calf pulled and had no desire to. Just thinking of someone reaching into the cow's uterus to hook chains to the calf's hooves gave her the heebie-jeebies. The next part would be worse, though. They'd attach the chains to a winch and then ratchet the baby out, little by little. Ouch.

They sped back to the house as quickly as the electric motor would take them. Dad was on his way out, carrying some coco coir bales to the greenhouse for Mom when they reached him.

"Number 2144 is in labor," Caleb said. "She looks distressed. You need to come and check her."

"Jan, take these bales over to the greenhouse for me." Dad handed them to her. "Then go back to the house and tell your mother where I've gone and help her with the outdoor work today. Got it?"

She hopped out of the cart, Caleb slid to the passenger seat, and Dad took over the driver's spot. After watching them take off toward the pasture, she strode to the greenhouse to deposit the bales.

The greenhouse's automated fans were running, so it'd be at least the ninety-degree minimum to set them off. Opening the door brought a wave of heat and beads of sweat to her forehead. Not good. She propped the door with a bucket of potting soil to let more of the hot air mix with the cooler air outside.

This would not be fun.

Trudging back to the house, she met Mom in the carport, headed toward the greenhouse with her seed packets and liquid fertilizers in a garden tool bag.

"One cow is in labor. Dad and Caleb went to check it out, so I'm your assistant today." With a big smile, she tried to take the bag. The liquids could be heavy after a while.

"I've got it." Mom grasped the bag even harder and then strode toward the greenhouse. "Thank you, though."

Mom could be so stubborn sometimes. It was too humid for outside work today.

So Jan tried another tactic. "It's already pretty hot in the greenhouse, Mom. Maybe we should wait for tomorrow and get an earlier start."

"You don't have to help if it's too hot for you. I understand." Mom didn't even break stride.

"That's not what I meant, silly." *Try to keep the mood light. Try to help.* "What are we doing today?" She fell into step with Mom, sidestepping a nasty stickerweed.

"It's time to start the cabbage seeds. We're going to make sauerkraut this year."

When they entered the greenhouse, the heat had to be much higher than ninety, and sweat popped out on her brow. She needed to get the work knocked out since they wouldn't last long at this temperature. Picking up the potting soil bucket, she propped open the door to let more of the heat out.

She began setting up the assembly line so she could do most of the heavy work and run around while Mom sat and put seeds in the pots. But she soon realized the mistake of using the potting mix container to hold the door open. She'd have to either run fast to keep Mom seated or close the door to put the soil closer to the assembly line.

She scanned the area for something else to brace the door. Not much here. Then she spied a brick outside under a planter, snagged the block, and exchanged it for the potting soil container. But the door slowly closed since the brick wasn't heavy enough to keep it open.

Shoot.

"C'mon, kiddo," Mom said. "We won't be in here long. A little sweating won't kill us."

Maybe not me, but I don't know about you.

"Okay, let's hurry, though."

Jan lugged the potting mix next to the bench they'd be working on and filled the pots for the hydroponic tubes. As they had in the spring, she hustled to fill the pots with the mix to keep her mother busy planting the tiny seeds. After she had a line of pots waiting for her mother's touch, she hurried to Mom's other side to place the completed containers into the tubes.

Within minutes, the temperature rose again in the enclosed building. Jan kept popping over to the door to push it open, but it always eased closed again. Sweating profusely, she sure wished she'd worn a headband to keep the stinging salt out of her eyes.

Mom's face was beet red, and her shirt front had a V-shaped sweat pattern at the top, with the bottom of it soaked and filthy from where she'd pulled it up to wipe at her face. The stain on its back revealed how much fluid her body had given up.

It was too stinking hot in there for this.

"Why don't we take a break and finish up later?"

Mom didn't even look up. "It'll only get hotter. Let's get it finished."

Stubborn. Ugh.

Jan tried to pick up her speed, but with the air so humid, it was like slogging against a heavy curtain you couldn't get past. "Mom, I've got to take a break. This is crazy. Just a half-hour water break in the house?"

Mom made eye contact. Her face had gone pale instead of

the red it had earlier. "You go ahead, sweetie. I'll wait here for you. Give me a chance to catch up." Her weak smile caused the hairs on Jan's arms to rise.

She had to do something before Mom passed out.

"I don't feel so good, Mom. Can you please walk back with me?"

Mom's brow furrowed, bringing her forehead lines out on the pale skin. "I'm sorry. I didn't know. Of course." She rose from the stool and wavered on her feet.

Jan grabbed her arm to steady her and cringed at how cool and clammy her skin was. Not good.

"I guess I'm a little light-headed myself." Mom braced a hand on the counter before her, drawing in a shaky breath. "Maybe a break would be good for both of us." She took a few tentative steps toward the exit and then crumpled.

"Mom!" Jan grasped her mother's frail arms, helping her to the cement floor. "Mom... Talk to me... Are you okay?"

She moved her hand to her mom's wrist and felt her pulse— fast. Too fast. Why hadn't she insisted they take a break sooner?

Moving behind her mother's head, she grasped under her arms and dragged her out the door. Although the temperature was a little cooler outside, it wouldn't be nearly enough to cool Mom down. Feeling light-headed and queasy after the effort, Jan kneeled beside her and put her hand on the too-white cheeks. "Mom, can you hear me?"

Mom's eyes fluttered open. "Sorry... tired... minute." Then the eyes closed again.

Not good. I need to get her to the house, but if I pass out, we're both toast. "Rest for a minute, Mom. I'll be right back." No response.

Dragging herself to her feet, Jan started toward the house. She stumbled a few times, and it felt like miles, even though it was only a few hundred yards. When she arrived, she staggered in. The cool air stung her skin as though it was freezing the sweat onto her body. Shivers ran down her arms.

It raised her hopes that all would be okay as she moved through the house and out the front door to the porch where the bell hung. The clangor seemed too high to reach with her leaden arms, but she grasped it and used everything she had to ring the bell. She tried to hit it quickly so Dad and Caleb would understand the urgency, but it sounded languid to her ears. Over and over, she struck the triangle. Even if it sounded slow, the number of clangs would tell them something was wrong.

I need to get back to Mom. Back inside the kitchen, she snagged a handful of towels from the drawer. She moved over to the sink and turned on the water and put the towels under the flow. It felt so good. She shoved her arms into the water, then bowed her head, and allowed it to fall into the stream.

No! Can't stay. Mom needs this too. After turning off the water, she didn't wring the excess out of the towels, simply hustled to the door, allowing the water to run all over the floor as she moved. The water had revived her, but she still felt weak and nauseated.

No matter. She'd be fine.

Opening the carport door allowed a wave of heat to hit her face. What had they been thinking working in the greenhouse in these temperatures? One foot in front of the other, step after step, she reached her mother.

"Mom. You awake?" Jan kneeled beside the soaking-wet, pallid body. "I brought some cool towels for you." She placed a dripping cloth on her mom's face, and then pulled up her shirt and pressed a towel on her upper and then another on her lower torso. She only had one left, so she used it to wipe down Mom's arms.

"Um... thank... nice." Mumbling barely audible words, at least she was alert enough to speak. That had to be a good sign, right?

Where was Dad? Caleb? Hadn't it been hours since she'd rung the bell? Had they heard it? Maybe Jan just imagined ringing it. She put her forehead down on the towels. They were wet, but hot now. She swabbed her own face and arms to revive her sleepy self. Lying down beside her mother sounded so good. But she couldn't. Someone had to get Mom inside. If it were Mom kneeling here instead of her, she'd be praying.

"God, I need your help. Please. I need Mom to be okay."

Or maybe she should rest, just for a minute. Then she'd have enough strength to go again to ring the bell. So tired.

Chapter Ten

"Jan! Mom! Where are you?"

It sounded muffled—far away. She sat up—must have fallen asleep.

"Jan! Mom!"

Caleb, by the house.

She had to get his attention. "Caleb, over here."

The words sounded strange. Was she talking out loud?

"Hello. Is anyone around?"

He hadn't heard her. *Must yell louder.*

"Caleb." It still sounded wrong.

A door slammed shut. He must have gone inside. *No, we're out here.*

Mom—How was Mom? The towel was over her face. Jan slid it up so it no longer covered her eyes. "Mom, we need to get up and go back to the house. I don't feel so good."

Mom's eyes fluttered open, but then squinted shut again. "Ugh, too bright."

What a relief.

"Sorry, you scared me. You passed out. I fell asleep for a bit. Can you sit up?"

The house door slammed again.

"Mom! Jan!"

Okay, everything you've got this time. "Over here!"

Soon the golf cart puttered along, then crested the hill, heading toward them. *Oh, thank you, God!*

"Come on. Let's get you sitting up." Jan crawled to her mom's head, put her hands behind Mom's shoulders, and gave a good push to help her up. Mom eased into a sitting position.

Mom lifted her hand to press her temple. "My head... I'm going to be sick."

Caleb pulled up beside them and jumped out of the driver's seat. "What happened? Are you okay, Mom?"

"She collapsed on the way back from the greenhouse. Help me get her to the house." Jan grasped the golf cart beside her and hauled herself to her feet. Her eyes went out of focus, and the world spun around her.

"You don't look so good yourself. You'd better have a seat. I'll help Mom up."

After a moment or two, the spinning stopped, and the wooziness passed enough for her to move to a seat on the cart and pull herself up into it while Caleb hefted Mom to her feet. Mom just kept holding her head. *I'll bet her head's even dizzier than mine right now.*

"Where's your father?" Mom asked Caleb after she sat in the cart.

"Pulling a calf. Let's get you back in the house."

They drove the short distance, and Caleb helped Mom inside. Meanwhile, Jan rose, head whirling, and staggered in on her own.

With Mom sitting at the kitchen counter, Caleb gathered glasses, then filled each from the faucet before shutting off the flow. "Have a seat." He motioned Jan to a barstool, then tipped it to face the counter and placed glasses in front of her and

Mom. Next, he ran two tea towels under the water and wrapped one around each of their necks. "Drink up." He rubbed their shoulders. "I'm going for a thermometer."

As he dashed away, her hands didn't want to move. The glass weighed a ton, and she used both hands to pick it up so she didn't drop it. After she got about a third of the water down, she wobbled the glass back to the counter. Mom drank some of her water but kept her eyes closed. The pale look transformed into a reddened face again. That had to be another good sign.

Rapid footfalls rushed back, and Caleb arrived with a thermometer.

"Open up." He stood between her and Mom and pointed the old-fashioned mercury device at Mom's mouth. She complied and waited for the reading. After a minute, he removed the thermometer. "Hmm… 102.3 degrees… Drink more water. I'll start a cool bath for you."

Caleb shook the thermometer, then held it to Jan. "Next."

She opened her mouth and accepted the cool glass under her tongue, clamping down to hold it in place. While she waited for it, Caleb got another set of towels and ran cool water over them. He came back around the counter again, replaced the one on Mom's neck with the fresh towel, then did the same for Jan.

He headed toward their parents' bedroom. Soon the beckoning sound of water running drifted out, so he must have started the cooling bath. Then, once again, he was beside her and sliding the thermometer out of her mouth. He tipped it to find the reading. "Aha, 101.6—not as bad, but I'll bet you have a good headache anyway, huh?"

She nodded and regretted the motion.

"I'm going to help Mom get to her bath. Then I'll get yours started."

"I can get to the bath on my own." Mom turned on the seat as if to rise and then paused, putting her hand on the raised wooden counter. "Well, maybe just a little help to the bathroom."

He offered his arm for Mom to grasp and snugged his other hand under her armpit to help her off the stool. Mom wobbled, and they shuffled to the master bedroom. Then came Mom's muffled voice. "Okay, I'm fine. Thank you. Go help your sister."

Soon, the faint sound of water running sloshed in the bathroom tub Jan and Caleb shared upstairs. More quick footsteps, and he was beside her again.

"Why don't you finish up that glass of water before we head to our bathroom?"

She picked it up and polished off the water. "I could drink a gallon."

"Best take it slowly. The last thing I want to have to do is clean up vomit." He stuck his finger into his open mouth as if to gag himself and rolled his eyes up.

"Goofball."

"At least I know when to take a break and get a drink. Shall we?" He put his arm out to her as if offering her a dance.

She took the proffered arm and eased to her feet. The spinning sensation returned. Still, she let him guide her to their bathroom. She released his arm only after he installed her on the edge of the half-filled tub. "Thanks."

"It's going to feel cold because your body is so hot. So suck it up, Buttercup. I made the water warm enough to avoid too much of a shock, but cool enough to cool you down. I'll wait outside the door for a few minutes. Holler when you are in the tub."

He left the room, closing the door behind him with a soft click. She struggled to pull off her sodden shirt with her noodle arms. Her ponytail tangled in the collar, and she wrested it free. After the ordeal of freeing her body from her clothing, she slid one foot into the water.

Yup, stinkin' cold.

Had he been honest about it being tepid, or was he waiting outside the door to hear her holler about the ice bath he'd prepared? She forced herself to put the other foot into the water and then slid off the side of the tub and into the bath. *Brrrr.*

"I'm in, and it's freezing. I hope you're happy."

"As a lark. I'm checking on Mom. Then I'll check with you one more time before I go check on Dad."

She heard him stepping away from the door. After adjusting to the temperature, she used a washcloth to rinse her body off. This could have ended up worse—a lot worse.

«»

By the time she got out of the tub and dressed in dry clothing, Dad and Caleb were in the kitchen talking. She was so thirsty she might just drink the well dry. On the dining room side of the kitchen, Caleb had braced both elbows behind him on the marble countertop, studying her approach as she crossed the open floor plan rooms. So she tucked damp tendrils of red hair away from her face and asked what she had to know. "How's Mom doing?"

"She's going to be okay, thanks to this guy." Dad jabbed a fist at Caleb's arm. "Good job remembering the heat exhaustion protocols."

Dad was soaking wet and filthy. Mud and blood covered his shirt. He held a half-consumed glass of water and smelled of manure and perspiration. "How are you feeling, Jan?"

She edged around them into the kitchen and reached into the cupboard and pulled down a plastic mug. "I'm thirsty and tired but feel much better than I did when Caleb found us."

Better not to risk my shaky hands with something breakable.

She moved to the refrigerator and filled her mug from the dispenser. The ice maker had broken last year, and no parts were available for repairs. She was too tired to bother digging ice out of the freezer.

Turning to her brother, she hoisted her mug in a weak salute. "I hate to admit it, but you saved our butts out there. I didn't know how to get Mom home. I waited too long to insist she come in."

After she seated herself at the counter, Dad gave her a side hug. "I'm glad Caleb found you when he did. Good idea to ring the bell."

"How's the new mama and baby? They both make it?"

"We were lucky this time. She's a first-time heifer and had trouble. The calf looks small, probably premature. We'll need to keep a close eye on them, so I put them in the pen for a few days."

She laughed as he pulled away from her. "That's good, but you don't smell so nice."

"Sorry. I'm letting your mom finish up, and then I'll get into the shower. In fact, let me go check on her now. She was close to being done a few minutes ago." He walked toward the converted master bedroom, paused, and glanced back at Caleb. "Can you handle starting supper?"

"It may be cowboy cornbread, but I'll figure out something." Caleb flashed a grin.

And her stomach rumbled. Cowboy cornbread may be an

easy-fix dinner, but with cooked ground beef, corn, and peppers as the base all mixed in with cornbread batter, it sounded heavenly. As a special treat, he'd add cheese when it was available. But it had been a while since they'd had cheese. As it was, they only used half of the beef in it that they used to.

She braced her chin in her hands as her brother rummaged around. Wow, he was almost an adult now—more than almost. At eighteen, he was technically an adult for most purposes. She'd never thought of him that way, though. He was just her big brother.

«»

"You feel up to checking on that new calf with me?" Caleb nudged her at the kitchen table the next morning.

The metal chair rocked beneath her as she yawned. She'd slept hard, not getting up once despite all the water she'd consumed during the evening. "Sure. How did Baby look last night when you checked?"

"He was curled up when I checked on him. Mama was eating just fine. I haven't seen him nurse yet, though."

They headed to the carport and tugged on their boots. Nursing could be a problem for a new mother. Not all cows took to it naturally, and some just didn't take the best care of their babies.

She paused before opening the door. "Should we take a bottle, just in case?"

"I don't want to waste any formula. We don't have much left."

Right. There was never much of anything left these days. If they couldn't grow, raise, or make it, it would be in short supply.

Dad said he was going to look for a few more milk cows in

the spring since formula was so scarce. They'd need a truck to pick one up, wouldn't they?

They drove the cart to the corral. When they arrived, the baby bull was standing on tiny legs. Jet-black, just like his mama and papa, he looked too small to reach his mother's udders to eat. The little guy was bawling his head off. Mama was ignoring him.

"That can't be good." Caleb freed a hand from the steering wheel to tug at his hair. "Better head back and get a bottle."

He spun the cart around as she resisted an "I told you so." Instead, she squirmed in her seat. After her head hurt so yesterday, the rushing in her ears had taken hours to settle. But she could almost swear she now heard—a rumbling? A vehicle?

"Caleb?"

"Yep. I hear it too." He nodded toward their dirt driveway and the dust kicking up. "Someone's coming."

He parked in front of the house, and they waited.

Finally, a police truck came into view. Officer Bradley from the auction got out as Dad exited the house. He joined Jan and Caleb while the officer approached.

Dad offered his hand to shake. "Afternoon. What brings you out?"

"I bring you good news, of a sort. But these days, good news always seems to accompany the bad." He ground his boot heel into the gravel, then shot a sideways glance at her. "You may want this conversation to be private."

"Go get the bottle, Jan," Dad said.

"But—"

Dad shot her The Look—no use. She shuffled to the house. Dad hadn't made Caleb leave. Not fair.

"Who's here?" Mom asked as she entered the kitchen.

"Officer Bradley. He's got news he wouldn't say in front of me, so I get to make up a bottle for the new calf since he isn't nursing."

She wanted to kick something. Caleb was only two years older than she was. Why did she have to come in? *Probably because I'm the "little lady."* Disgusting.

Soon the door opened, and Dad came in. "I've got to head out with Officer Bradley, luv."

Mom shot out of her chair where she was darning socks. "What happened? What's wrong?"

He put out a hand to quiet her. "It's okay—some good news for a change. They found our truck." His face remained serious.

What? Was it possible the nightmare she'd created was over? But then Jan scrunched up her face. "But that's great news. Why couldn't I hear that?" Her heart was beating double time. The best news she'd heard in months. "Where is it?"

"Hold up. There was bad news too. Remember? They found a corpse in it."

Chapter Eleven

Dead? In their truck? Who? How? Jacob? With her head spinning from the news, Jan braced a hand on the nearest counter, the blue cupboards and brick backsplash swirling in her vision, the marble countertop cool beneath her palm. There was no love lost between her and the boy, but she didn't want him dead.

"How horrible." Mom pressed a hand to her chest. "Do they know who it was? Was it the boy?"

Dad shook his head. "No, it was an adult male. He had no ID on him, so they don't know who it was." He studied Jan before he went on. "But there were signs a boy had been living with the man."

Her legs wobbled as relief flooded her. She let out a breath she hadn't realized she'd been holding. Jacob wasn't dead.

Caleb came into the house.

Dad continued. "They appeared to be camping in the truck bed. They had a mattress and such. The guy's been dead for a while. They said I can have the truck back since they've removed the body. But I have to take gas with me and a tire. Apparently, it has a flat."

Mom moved over to her and put her arm around her. "It's an answer to prayer, isn't it?"

Jan shivered and leaned into Mom. Yes, she'd wanted the truck back more than anything. There had been times she wanted to wring Jacob's neck for stealing it. Now she wasn't sure how to feel. He was still a thief. Now he was also a child on his own.

"I'm heading out with Officer Bradley," Dad said. "Caleb, why don't you come along and help me get the tire changed out."

Caleb eyed her. "Are you good with feeding that calf by yourself?" It could be hard to get the newborn to take the bottle for the first time.

Mom chimed in. "I can help."

"You will do no such thing." Dad folded his arms across his chest and gave Mom The Look. "We discussed this. You're in the house for the week other than brief trips—no outside work. Remember?"

Her arm slid away from Jan as she crossed them to mimic his stance. "I'm not an invalid."

"We could've lost you, and you know it." He walked over and pulled her into an embrace.

Jan cringed. *Okay, enough of the mushy stuff.*

"And I'm not an idiot." Hands on her hips, Jan glared at them all. "I can make a bottle and feed a calf, for crying out loud."

True, she'd fed calves, but this would be her inaugural attempt to train one to take his bottle. How hard could it be, anyway? If her brother could manage it, she could. Difficulty-wise, it couldn't compare to the pyramids she and the other cheerleaders concocted. Just because she'd planned a big advertising career, not a life on the farm, didn't mean they had a right to act like she was an imbecile around here.

"All right then." Dad gave Mom one last hug and kissed her

forehead. "Caleb, go grab the spare tire for the truck. I'm going to get some gas, and we're off."

Though Mom had stood statue-still for the first embrace, she put her arms around him for the second and squeezed before he headed toward the door.

"Hustle, Caleb. I don't want to make Officer Bradley wait any longer."

"Yes, sir."

«◇»

With the large bottle of warm calf formula in her hand, Jan stepped into the corral and eyed the new baby and mama. Her plan of attack ready, she spoke soothingly to the pair. "Morning, Mama. Morning, Baby. I've got some nice warm milk."

The cow eyed her and continued to munch on hay. The baby lay curled up in a ball about one hundred yards away. Jan crept toward the young calf while keeping a close eye on its mother. Thankfully, the calf was far enough away from its mama for Jan to get in between the two with plenty of distance from a potentially angry parent.

Mama would naturally protect her calf from the human who appeared to be stalking her baby. Though since she wasn't properly feeding her calf, the cow might not have the instinct to protect it either. As Jan approached the baby, it wobbled to its feet and moved away from its pursuer.

"Yes, perfect. Keep going, little one."

Staying behind the baby, she maneuvered it into a smaller part of the corral area where she could corner it. As the calf passed through a gate, she closed the entrance behind her. Now, even if the calf's mother changed her mind about wanting to protect the little one, she couldn't get in to interfere. All Jan had to do was corner the bugger.

"Come on, fellow. You're going to like this, I promise." She kept her voice low with a singsong tone.

It didn't take long to corral the calf. Because the little guy hadn't eaten properly, it had scant energy to run. In a smaller area, she proffered the bottle.

"Look what I've got. You're hungry, right? It's yummy."

The baby moved away.

Maybe it needed to smell the formula.

She moved closer to the calf again, expressed some of the liquid onto its muzzle, then tried again to put the bottle into the tiny mouth. "Hey, buddy, taste this. You're hungry, right?"

Again, the baby moved away.

She didn't have all day here.

"All right, kiddo. We can do this the easy way or the hard way. You're about to learn the hard way if you don't drink this bottle."

She cornered the baby again. This time, she straddled the fellow with his head poking out from between her jean-clad legs, his body behind her. She put the bottle down to his mouth and forced his jaws apart, thrusting in the nipple before he could close them again.

He chewed on the nipple once... twice... and then spit it out, twisting his muzzle away. He tried to back away, but she clamped her legs around his neck, pinning him there while struggling to keep her balance. Amazing how strong a little calf could be. Even a premature newborn was nearly too strong to hold.

"Almost. You're so close. Let's try this again."

Once again, she pried his mouth open, pushed in the bottle, and then squeezed as hard as she could to force some of the formula into his mouth. He swallowed the liquid, then clamped onto the nipple and sucked.

"Yes! There you go, buddy."

Since he'd figured out how to suckle, the calf nursed greedily. He would butt the bottle occasionally, making it hard to hold on. Once it was empty, she pulled the nipple away.

"All gone, baby. Sorry. Let's let that milk settle in your tummy."

As she walked toward the gate, the calf followed, butting her with its head, trying to get more milk.

"No. We don't want to make you sick with too much. I'll be back later with more."

The calf followed her past the gate and into the main corral where the cow continued to munch. Jan ended up sprinting to make it to the corral exit gate ahead of the demanding calf. She opened the gate, slid through, and closed it before the baby could escape. It stopped and bleated at her.

"You almost got me, but I'm still faster than you. Maybe not for long, but for today." She couldn't help but grin at the determination the small bull showed.

Mission accomplished.

As she headed back to the house with the empty bottle, she remembered Jacob and the dead adult. A lump formed in her throat. Here she was dealing with a minor problem, a wrinkle in her otherwise protected life. Meanwhile, Jacob was out there, alone now.

What did that mean? If he showed up today, would she treat him any differently? Perhaps the dead body in the truck wasn't even his relation. There might be more than one adult he worked with. Just because he was a kid didn't mean she could trust him.

Fool me once, shame on you. Fool me twice, shame on me.

Wasn't that from a movie? She didn't remember, but it was a good saying, nonetheless. She had fallen for his game once. It wouldn't happen again.

«»

She was baking her drop biscuits to accompany Mom's chicken stew for supper when they heard the popping of gravel in the driveway. She ran to the front window, breathing out a release of months' anxiety when their truck finally came home. Although filthy, the vehicle appeared undamaged from where she stood.

Did they go mudding in the truck or what?

She dashed across the room, out the door, and waited for them to pull up to the house. Dad and Caleb stepped out and shut the doors behind them.

"Well?" she asked. "Is it okay? Any damage?"

Dad pulled her into a hug when he reached her. "Just the flat tire and empty gas tank. Other than that, she needs a bath, inside and out. We're back in business."

The weight that had clung to her for weeks fell away. Feeling light again, she closed her eyes and breathed in deeply, imagining the air filling her lungs lifting her up like a helium balloon.

Thank you, God, for bringing it back to us. I promise never to be an idiot again.

"Supper's almost ready. It's your favorite, big brother." She winked at Caleb. "Chicken stew over biscuits."

"I'm so hungry I could eat a raw bird at this point. Let's eat."

«»

Having gotten so used to the long drive in the golf cart, she'd forgotten the truck would get them to the auction in half an hour. Not only that, but they could bring their large table and more goods. But the best part was the trailer they towed behind them, carrying six steers. Finally.

As she stepped down from the truck's running board, she took in the sounds of the lowing cattle and the scent of their dung. What heaven to experience a real auction day again, at last.

"Don't wander off, Jan," Dad said. "After we offload these steers, I'll drop you and Mom off to get the table set up."

"Yes, sir." She had a few minutes for him to get checked in with the auction barn and unload. While she waited, she surveyed the animal pens. When she was little, they'd only sold cattle at the barn. Now you could purchase sheep, goats, and donkeys. Smaller animals were available at the booths set up around the auction. The combination of so many animals created a raucous sound and a powerful assault on the nose.

The scent brought back a flash of memory. Renee hadn't yet moved to Columbus, and she'd come to auction day with Jan and the family. They'd stood here, at the pens, reaching to pet the young calves for sale. So many little ones together in one place, loud and exciting. The adolescent animals would look for food handouts as they passed by.

They had developed a silly game—Name That Cow. She chuckled, remembering how they came up with names. A white forehead became "Cloud," a brown tail was "Caramel," and a set of patches down the side became "Spot."

She missed having a friend along. She'd rarely been alone on auction day. Even if Renee couldn't tag along, Jan ran into other school friends here and there. But most of them had moved to the city.

"Hi, Jan." That voice, oh no!

Spinning around, she scowled at Lizzy. *Why her? Pretend you didn't hear her.*

"Hey, didn't you hear me? Probably not. It's kind of loud here, huh?" Lizzy stepped up next to her at the corral and nudged her shoulder. "What a smell. Whew! Glad I don't have to clean those pens. You ever have to clean a pen? I haven't. Never been on a farm until we moved out to the country. I bet I could, though, you know? It can't be that hard, right?"

More vomiting of words. Would she ever stop? Jan glared at the chatterbox.

Give her the silent treatment. The girl couldn't be dumb enough to miss the meaning. Turning back to the animals, Jan rested her arms on the corral rails, wishing the invader away.

"Aw, come on. Talk to me. Don't you need a friend?" Lizzy moved even closer, pushing her arm up against Jan. "I need one. Please speak to me. Please?"

Okay, now she was getting whiny. That high-pitched pleading was beyond annoying. Time to see if Dad's ready to go. "Later."

Jan rushed back to the truck, thankful to see him shaking hands with the auction owner, sealing the deal. Caleb was shutting the back of the now-empty trailer. Hallelujah. Time to go. She yanked open the truck door, climbed in, and shut it as if Lizzy were a demon chasing her. As she looked back, Lizzy was chasing her with her eyes—a sad-puppy look, if Jan had ever seen one. No matter—best Lizzy didn't like her, anyway. Jan wouldn't trust her any more than she did any other stranger.

After Dad got the truck parked, they unloaded the table and material swatches, canned vegetables, beef jerky, and whittled items to sell and trade. It was good to be able to carry everything again. It meant two people would need to man the larger offering, though. One person couldn't watch it all, and they couldn't afford to lose any of it to thieves.

"I'll take the first watch with Mom, Squirt." Caleb slapped her back. "You see what's good in trade. Just don't forget to spell me after lunch."

"Appreciate it. I won't be out long. You need extra visiting time today, huh?" She winked at him. Somewhere around the auction was a pretty blonde he'd search diligently for.

Jan stuck to the edges of the crowd and piddled around with a stop to pet soft rabbits. As she meandered, she inhaled the scents of salty buttered popcorn at one booth and ogled the homemade jewelry at another. Who would spend hard-earned money or trade food for these items? Yes, they were pretty, but where did anyone have to go to dress up?

Halfway around, she headed back to relieve Caleb. It was always worth having him owe her a favor. Then she saw Lizzy coming her way. Shoot. She dodged left, toward the outside of the crowd. Head low, she slunk toward their table, alert to avoid making contact.

Intent on avoiding the girl, she ran straight into a small person, knocking him down. *Oof.* Her feet tangled in a blanket that smelled as if something had died in it. *Ugh.*

"I'm so sorry. Let me help you up." She drew back the offensive covering to find a filthy face looking back at her. Jacob.

Chapter Twelve

As Jan disentangled herself from the blanket, Jacob's eyes grew wide. He scrambled to his feet and took off running, leaving the blanket behind. She froze, but recovered and charged off in pursuit. At least that was her goal, but her feet tangled in the blanket still surrounding them and tripped her again. She stumbled and dropped to a knee.

"Shoot. Jacob, come back here!" Grabbing for the blanket, she freed her feet, took his covering with her despite the stench, and sprinted after him. "Jacob. Stop!"

He was smart. Instead of heading toward the woods, he dove into the crowd. Under tables, around obstacles, and through tiny passages only a smaller child could navigate, he led her on a chase. She could hear him cough. Was he sick?

She stopped and threw the blanket to the ground. Who knew what germs it might contain? Perhaps even the variant. Ahead, he crawled under the cattle trailer blocking their pathway. He scuttled to the other side so quickly that, by the time she reached the trailer and stooped to peer under it, he'd vanished. *Shoot. Lost him again.*

What should she do? She could go around the trailer and try to find him or return to their table to relieve Caleb as planned. And what was that smell? She lifted her hands to her nose and sniffed. Ugh. Whatever had been on the blanket was now on her.

Let him run. They had the truck back, anyway. Catching him wouldn't change anything for them. It would just keep him from stealing from anyone else. Of course, most people were smarter than she had been. She was smarter now too. Good riddance.

«»

The successful auction day not only had the steers sell at a good price but also allowed Dad to buy a magnificent bull with a solid pedigree. His calves, small at birth, had rapid growth. They brought back few of their canned goods, but a generous portion of wheat flour and golden honey. Mom had negotiated for some sorghum plants she'd been eyeing. With those, they could grow their own sweeteners. A successful day, indeed.

Strangely though, while she and Caleb were packing things up for the trip home, Dad had been whispering with Mom behind the truck. Curiosity gnawed at Jan. With Dad's face solemn and Mom's eyes tearful, it must be serious.

"Everything okay?" Jan asked as they settled into the truck.

"Yes, good day," Dad said.

Mom faced her window and said nothing.

"That bull will get the second herd off to a good start." Dad drummed his hands on the steering wheel, a pep to his voice. "Now we can keep our heifers and move them between the two herds. It'll be a snap to expand onto the Boswell farm now."

That grabbed her attention. "The Boswell property?"

"Yes, Mr. Boswell and I agreed I'd lease his south fields once we had enough for the second herd." He smiled at her through the rearview mirror.

Her heart lurched, and she couldn't help scooting forward,

115

straining against her seat belt. "Does that mean they can move back now? Is he going into business with you?"

"I don't know about that. We agreed to this years ago, before he left. I doubt what I pay him would be enough for them to give up work in the city."

"Oh." Hope shriveled and died in her chest, sinking to land like a stone in her gut.

"Sorry, kiddo. You never know, though."

"Yeah." She no longer trusted in hopes and wishes. Exhausted from being alone. Done with having no one outside her family she could trust.

«»

At home, Dad went through his gun safe, pulling out ammo and guns, sorting through them, and then packing them all back in. Strange behavior. Something was up. Mom had been way too quiet cooking supper. Man, the grim atmosphere could use some music. How long before they spilled the beans?

Jan set the table, positioning hers and Caleb's metal chairs across from one another, and then went to the stove to stir the pinto beans as Mom made salad. "Something's wrong. What's going on?" It came out almost as a whisper, just the thought of what could be wrong stealing her breath away.

Mom merely smiled, but it didn't make her eyes glow. "I'm just thinking, sweetie."

"Uh-huh. And is Dad just thinking as he sorts through the gun safe?" Straight-A student, here, remember? Well, not counting those Cs in math. Surely, they didn't think she was stupid.

Mom frowned toward the safe before the plastered-on smile returned. "You know your dad. He likes to be prepared."

Yeah right. Time to press for answers. "For what?"

Dad walked in and made eye contact with Mom. "Caleb!" The bellow meant business. "Dinner. Now!"

Quick steps of socked feet thudded down the stairwell. Caleb turned the corner with a grin. "Don't have to call me twice for dinner. I'm famished."

"Sit down. We need to talk before we eat," Dad said.

This couldn't be good.

Mom turned off the pinto beans and lifted the cornbread out of the oven before she joined them, already seated at the table.

Dad covered Mom's hand as she sat. Huh, it was shaking. "I heard some concerning news at the auction today. Apparently, a group of men has been raiding homes between here and Columbus. They're stealing food, gas, money—whatever they can lay their hands on." He paused and squeezed Mom's hand, but she pulled her hand away and rested it in her lap, focusing on the table.

"I asked Officer Bradley, and he told me the gang shot a man who caught them in his house."

Jan gasped and covered her mouth. Her insides swirled like she might get sick. "Who, Dad? Who got shot?"

"I don't know, someone in Ellerslie." He made eye contact with her, then Caleb. A muscle twitched in his grim-set jaw. "We need to be prepared to protect our farm and ourselves."

A tear escaped Mom's left eye before she swiped it away.

Jan's heart pumped faster. That explained Dad's ammo check. Her mind froze at the thought of ammunition and guns. After the mental pause, questions flooded her mind. "What are we going to do? The dogs are already patrolling the fences every day." She twisted her hands together in her lap. "When Lizzy crossed onto our property, they had her cornered before she was even fifty yards from the fence."

"The dogs can't guard the entire property all the time." Caleb was tugging at his hair. "It's too big. Someone could watch for when they do their runs and avoid them."

Dad nodded. "We'll need to add our own patrols to help the dogs cover the property."

Mom's head snapped up. "Absolutely not. My babies are not patrolling with loaded guns."

"Marie, we talked about this." Dad reached out to cover Mom's hand again, but she wrenched it out of reach. The ferocious mama bear had awakened and now glared at him.

"You know how I feel." Mom stood and pushed her chair away from the table. "Now you all know how I feel. God wouldn't want us to be arming our children. Where is your faith, Steve? It's gotta be there, no matter how far down you bury it." She stalked toward the master bedroom. "I'm not hungry anymore. It's your turn to clean up after supper, Jan."

The door clicked shut behind her.

Shock overwhelmed Jan. She'd never seen her parents argue. Whenever they disagreed on something, they took it behind closed doors and emerged in agreement.

"Sorry, guys." White-faced, Dad stood and pushed his own chair back. "Your mom's struggling with our new reality. I thought we'd had it worked out. Eat supper. It'll be okay." His shoulders drooped as he followed her path. With a single knock at the bedroom door, he opened it, entered their sanctuary, and closed them in.

Heat burned Jan's eyes. Everything was falling apart. This was so much worse than missing her friends or feeling lost without her art and career. A strangled sound escaped.

Caleb walked around the table. He pulled her chair out and kneeled in front of her, raising her chin with his hand. "Come on, Squirt. It's going to be okay. They'll figure it out. We're Worthingtons, and Worthingtons stick together. You know that."

Only when he enveloped her in a hug did she allow herself to draw comfort from his strength.

«»

They ate supper together. Or at least she pushed food around her plate while Caleb ate. Mom and Dad stayed in their bedroom, mumbles of conversation leaking out, but not much else. After they had finished, Jan got up to clear the table.

Caleb stepped into her path and winked with a grin. "Want to have a contest?"

The twinkle in his eye was too inviting to pass up. "Let's hear it."

"I'll bet you I can have the leftover food packed up, put away, and the serving dishes in the dishwasher before you can load the plates and silverware. You also have to wipe down the table and stove. I'm willing to place a wager on it as well."

Now, this was interesting. "What are you willing to bet?"

"The next two nights when it's my turn to do the dishes against your next two nights."

Caleb hated doing cleanup, and he was slow as a sloth on vacation.

"I'll take your bet, sir. You better get your sneakers laced because I will have no mercy on you." She grinned, anticipating his defeat.

"Ready?" he asked.

"Set," she said.

"Go!" they both yelled and then jumped into action.

They tore into their tasks so fast that a fork went flying off the plate she snagged too quickly off the table. He sprinted toward the cupboard with a casserole dish, yanked open the cabinet door, and snatched a bowl with a lid. A second lid went flying.

She snagged the runaway silverware off the floor, and dishes clattered and clinked as she rushed between the table and the washer, loading it with unrinsed items. He scooped leftovers into disheveled piles, smashing lids on top to force food into containers not exactly the right size.

They turned to sprint back to the table and collided, bouncing off each other's shoulders, then erupting in laughter. Back and forth, they went, sliding on the shiny wood floors in their socked feet until she swiped the counter with the dishcloth and hollered, "Done!"

He was in midmotion to open the refrigerator door with his last bowl of food. His shoulders slumped. "Crap."

They broke out in laughter. She laughed so hard her ribs hurt and tears streamed down her face. He shoved the last bowl in the refrigerator and then knocked elbows with her on his way to sit at the table. The movement reminded her of the ruined family dinner and ended her giggles.

The master bedroom door opened, and Dad stepped out, his face taut until he focused on them. His pasted-on smile wouldn't convince anyone.

"Your mom just needs a minute. But she's fine." He rubbed his hands together in a let's-get-at-this gesture. "Any leftovers?"

"Plenty. In the fridge," Caleb said.

While Dad moved to the refrigerator, made himself a plate of food, and set it in the microwave to rewarm, Jan studied him for some sort of sign everything would be all right. If she searched intently, she'd find it—wouldn't she?

An opening door drew her attention back to the master bedroom. Mom exited, her face tear-blotchy. Realizing they watched her, she gave her a weak smile. It didn't help.

When Mom made her way to the table, Jan took her seat. Her stomach was so overwhelmed she might vomit.

Dad pulled his meal from the microwave. "Would you like me to warm you a plate, luv?"

"No thank you. I'm good."

At the table, Dad brushed his hand over Mom's shoulder and squeezed before he took his seat. "We're sorry to have argued in front of you two." He looked at each of them. "Our intention is never to bring you into any of our disagreements. I thought we had it worked out, but we didn't quite. We do now."

He then made eye contact with Mom, who nodded.

"Yes. We have a plan."

Chapter Thirteen

The sign was as straight as possible in the ground—wasn't it? Jan stepped back and eyed the writing again:

No Trespassing

If You Can Read This Sign

You Are in Range

"Dad, is this good enough?" She had to yell to get his attention.

"Looks good. Now come help your brother."

A rough sketch of a pistol completed the message. She still had to giggle at the wording, even though it was stone-cold serious. She collected the drill and hammer she'd used to install the sign, then returned to where Dad and Caleb were working. "Why didn't we just put it at the end of the driveway instead of halfway down it?"

"Well, that's a point of contention between your mother and me." Dad stretched fishing line across the drive. He'd tied the end of the line to a tree on the opposite side. "I didn't want a sign at all. No one should be on our property."

He reached the other side and tied it to a gadget bolted to an opposite tree. "But your mom wanted to be sure nobody got caught unaware. So, we compromised. Halfway down the driveway, where they shouldn't be anyway, we give them a warning not to go any farther."

"But why not warn people before they start down our road?"

"Because warning people not to come our way is telling them there is something of value down here. Not the message we want to send."

That made sense. "Oh."

She understood Mom's point too, though. There weren't many good options if the people who raided homes came their way.

After he finished tying the fishing line to the contraption, the line stretched six inches above the ground and almost disappeared to the naked eye. "Okay, I'm going to arm it. Get back to the driveway and be mindful of the trip wire."

She moved to the middle of the driveway, far enough away to watch the next step. Caleb stepped up beside her as Dad fished a shotgun shell out of his pocket, slid it into the cylindrical trip alarm, then armed the spring. He backed away and surveyed his handiwork.

"I can still see the fishing line, Dad." Caleb tugged at his hair. "Are you sure this is going to work?"

"You can only see it because you know it's there." Dad stood between them and put his arm around each of their shoulders. "But someone who doesn't know to look out is going to trip over it, which is why it's called it a trip wire."

She couldn't imagine someone missing the line, but it might be hard to see if you weren't watching for it.

"When the line gets pulled, it triggers the shotgun shell, and the resulting shot gives us our warning to watch for the person heading our way."

A shiver tripped down her spine. "Will it hurt the person who sets it off?"

"They'd have to be right next to it for that to happen. No pressure behind the projectile means it won't go anywhere. But it'll scare the silly out of anyone who triggers it."

They stood there staring at their handiwork. All she could think were the what-if scenarios and the people she loved who were in danger.

"Next step, guys." Dad faced the house and swung a rope out of the golf cart. "Jan, start drilling the hole for that second sign your mom made. Caleb, with me."

Mom seemed so stressed when they explained the plan—a warning for anyone trespassing, then an alert for the family. Next, a second warning sign, and a weapon she hoped no one would ever set off.

Jan picked up the second sign from the cart, walked another hundred yards down the driveway, and drilled a second hole. Once she'd prepared the spot, she stuck the homemade sign in and gave it a few taps on top to ensure it was solid. Then she packed dirt in and around the sign. A good wiggle told her she'd done a fair job. It wasn't going anywhere. Rock-solid.

Reading this sign gave her chills:

Danger!

Final Warning

Turn Back Now

But Dad and Caleb were working further on down the driveway, and come to think of it, she'd better help. That log wasn't light. She trekked back to the cart, put her tools in, and drove down their half-mile driveway to where Dad and Caleb were tying a length of rope to one side of a huge log. It had to weigh at least five hundred pounds, and it blocked the driveway. She drove the cart off the drive and around the downed tree, then hopped out. "Sign's up. What's next?"

"Take the cart up and get the truck. Park it on the other side of this log," Dad said.

"Yes, sir."

Dad had taught her how to operate the vehicle a few years ago. Everyone had to pitch in where they were able. Driving a truck required very little muscle, so she often did the lighter chore while Caleb helped with the more challenging tasks.

After parking in the carport, she jogged into the house for the truck keys.

"Caleb? Is that you?" Mom asked from the kitchen.

"It's me, Mom. Caleb is out with Dad. I just needed the keys."

Mom's steps padded closer. Then her head popped around the corner, and she peered down the hallway. "Tell your father lunch will be ready in about thirty minutes, please."

"Yes, ma'am." Jan plucked the keys off the pegboard, jogged back out to the truck, jumped in, and drove down the drive, parking in front of the log.

They had dug some small trenches under the enormous log to run ropes under it. She joined them. They had cords attached to both ends of the log and looped over a huge tree limb towering above the driveway.

Dad took another section of rope, tied it to the center of the log, and then to the truck. "Okay, Caleb. Get in the truck and back it up. Slowly, son. Very slow."

As Caleb took over the steering wheel, backing up at a snail's pace, the log rose about four feet off the ground.

Dad put a fist in the air. "Hold."

He tightened both end ropes so the log could swing at the four-foot level. Caleb got out and untied the rope from the vehicle. He walked the rope end back down the driveway to a second overhanging limb, then tossed the rope until he swung it over the limb. They attached the rope to the truck to hoist the log into the trees, hidden from sight.

"You two need to be clear of this before I set the trigger," Dad said. "I don't want any chance one of you will set it off. It would crush the truck, and you'd be toast."

At least the dogs didn't patrol past here and wouldn't be setting it off—or so Dad had assured Caleb. She walked back toward the house, well out of reach of the log swing. Dad set the trigger and then a trip wire, which he disguised with leaves and limbs. He joined Caleb in the truck, then picked her up on their way back.

"Dad, what if a friend wants to come down the driveway? What if it's Officer Bradley or someone like that?"

"We've notified people that there is no trespassing. They take a risk whenever they ignore blatant warnings like ours." He didn't even turn to her to say this. "Times have changed, kiddo. We have to protect ourselves."

Back at the house, they trooped into the kitchen where Mom was finishing lunch.

"All done?" she asked.

"Done." Dad moved around the counter to kiss Mom on the cheek. "After we eat, we start some target practice."

Caleb's eyebrows shot up. "Do we have enough ammo for practice?"

"Not even close." Dad moved to wash his hands. "We're going to be working on penny exercises."

"Penny exercises?" Jan cocked her head to one side. She'd never heard of those. It sounded like something she could handle—nothing scary about coins.

A massive grin spread Dad's lips and crinkled up his cheeks as he reached for the towel and winked at her. "You'll see."

《》

"My arms are killing me." Jan flexed her fingers. Man, it had been too long since she'd gone to cheer practice and done such repetitive drills. "Haven't we practiced enough for one day?" Her arms felt like jelly. Granted, pom-poms were a lot lighter—and more fun—than rifles. She wanted so badly to put the wretched thing down, although she'd only been practicing for fifteen minutes.

"Hand it to your mother," Dad said.

Gratefully, Jan lowered the gun to the ground. The cleaning rod and penny fell to the dirt. "Here, Mom. All yours."

"Lovely." Mom gave her a wink. "Just what I've always wanted." Accepting the gun, she pointed it away from her family while she retrieved the cleaning rod and penny, inserted the rod, and snugged the gun to her shoulder. "Okay. Let's do this. Penny on."

When Jan put the penny on the end of the cleaning rod now protruding from the barrel, Mom aimed at the target on the other side of the yard and dry pulled the trigger.

The penny fell to the ground.

"Again," Mom said.

Jan stooped for the penny and placed it, once again, on the end of the cleaning rod. They repeated the process over and over—dry firing the gun with a spent shell in the chamber to prevent damaging the pin. After a while, her mom's arms drooped to a point where she could no longer line the target into her firing sights. She lowered the gun and scowled at Dad. "Remind me again why I'm doing this."

"Because you love your family." He slid the rifle from her hands. "We can't afford to burn through our ammo. And you, my love, don't want to kill anyone. Your best chance to keep your family alive without killing someone else is to practice. Aim well and let that dangerous person know you're not one to toy with."

"I get that." She rolled her eyes and rubbed the back of her neck. "But why am I dry firing at a target? How do I know I'm getting any better?"

He wrapped an arm around her and waved the rifle to point at the target. "You've already proven you can hit that target, right?"

Mom nodded.

"Then you need to be sure you can keep the rifle steady when you're firing. If you keep the penny steady while shooting, chances are, you're going to hit that target every time."

Mom sighed and eyed the target one more time. "I pray I never have to fire this gun at another human." She leaned into him and rested her head on his shoulder, closing her eyes as she let out a long low breath. "I don't think I could pull the trigger."

Amen. Jan frowned as they headed back for the house. *I don't think I could either.*

Chapter Fourteen

Everything hurt. At a minimum, she wouldn't be picking up a rifle for a month. At least she hoped so. Penny practice had done her in, and the hot shower had been heavenly. How did people manage without access to hot water? Did Renee have hot water? Lizzy definitely didn't.

Shaking away that thought, she plopped down on her bed, the plush duvet billowing up around her, and rubbed her wet hair with the towel. *Renee.* She hadn't checked her email this month. What were the chances her BFF had responded after all this time?

Why not? It could happen. She got back up on tired legs and forced her weak arms to lift the laptop. Then let it boot up while she slid into her pajamas.

Her arms wobbled while brushing her wet hair. Afraid she might drop the laptop, she returned to the bed and slid the device onto her lap. The web browser defaulted to her email, and the view of her inbox made her heart leap.

Jan:

I miss you, I miss you, I miss you! I'm sorry I didn't write back sooner. Daddy hasn't been able to find steady work, so we've all been pitching in doing odd jobs where we can. I've been crazy busy.

The hardest part is that Daddy's laptop broke, and we can't afford a new one. I met a really cute guy, though. His name is TJ, and he let me borrow his family's computer for a quick message. I've got to make this fast.

I have wonderful news. Daddy said we might move back to Shiloh soon. He figures we can do better hunting deer and growing our own crops than we're doing here in Columbus scavenging for jobs.

It's terrible here. You can't go out once the sun sets. We stay locked up all night in our apartment. You can hear gunshots all night long. It's like one of those old Westerns.

I hope to see you soon.

Your BFF,

Renee

Moving back? A squeal burst from Jan's throat, and she almost jostled the laptop. They might be neighbors again soon. Lizzy would be off that property, and Renee would be home. Jan slid the laptop back onto the bedside table and sprang out of bed, tired limbs forgotten.

"Mom! Dad!" she screamed and ran down to the living room where her parents sat on the canvas couch, bare feet resting on the pale brown area rug. As Dad jumped up and Mom's eyes went wide, Jan launched herself between them. "Guess what?"

"Whoa, girl, that smile could blind any fool who looked at it too long." Dad relaxed back on the couch. "Stop hopping around and just tell us."

"No, guess." She did a little jig and twirled.

Mom set her sewing aside and sat forward on the couch.

"Come on, sweetie. I could use some of those good vibes you've got going on there."

"They're coming back!" A screech escaped her lips.

"Who?" Mom and Dad asked in unison.

"Renee and her family. They can't find work, so they're coming home." Executing one of their old cheer moves, Jan jumped up and down in place with the intricate steps, unable to contain her joy.

"When?" Dad asked.

She froze. Hmm. She didn't know. She didn't even check how long ago Renee had sent the message. "Um, soon? Maybe. Renee just said soon."

"Well then, we'll have to keep an eye out for them." Mom rose from the couch, walked over, and hugged her. "I can't wait to see them all again."

But Jan wiggled free. "Wait, Dad, what about the driveway? What if they try to come down the drive? We need to pull that stuff back out."

"Negative." His jaw hardened. "We put that in place for a reason. It doesn't come down just because something positive happened. The danger still exists."

"But, Dad—" the look told her not to argue. She dropped her head to her chest while blood rushed through her ears. "Yes, sir."

But she couldn't let Renee or the Boswells get hurt. She. Just. Couldn't.

She dragged herself back into her bedroom, closed the door, and slumped against it. Then, needing it, she indulged herself by flicking on her butterfly lights. An LED glow lit the room with prisms of pinks and purples, blues and greens. She stepped over and slapped their dangling strings one at a time, sending each twinkling row fluttering, before opening the drawer she never let herself open. Closing her eyes, she stood there, seeing so much more than glittery tufts.

She'd email Renee and warn her not to come down the driveway. But what were the odds Renee would see it, and what about Max and Luna patrolling the fence lines—sugarplum fairies. There had to be a safe way to connect with her friend.

She fiddled with an old pom-pom. Just holding on to it usually brought a surge of inspiration—how else could she have come up with such great routines and even impressed the seniors? She lifted it to her face, breathing in the smell of the past, of normal, then laughed.

Aha! Renee's family would return to their home before coming to see them. All she had to do was leave a note at their house. Easy-peasy.

She waved the pom-pom over her head, giving a good all-out cheer for old times' sake as the excitement of her friend's return flowed through her. She wouldn't sleep a wink tonight. Jumping back into the bed, she again slid her laptop over and typed a response to Renee, letting her know she couldn't wait to see her. Since they didn't have a laptop anymore, Renee likely wouldn't ever see the message, but Jan at least had to try to tell her BFF she was waiting for her.

After tucking the laptop back safely on the desk, she cuddled up with a book, *Friends Surround Me*. While butterflies fluttered over her head and dreams danced in her heart, it was easy to fall into the fantasy of having friends all around her. But soon, the weariness caught up with her, and she had to turn off the lamp and give in.

«»

The note was simple—*R. Pay attention to the signs. They are*

132

real. I'll keep checking for you. J.

Luna and Max trotted alongside Jan as she walked through the pasture toward the fence splitting their farm from the Boswells' property line. She and Renee used to have a well-worn path between the two homes. Wild briars and saplings had since taken over. She passed through the gate Dad had put in the fence for them. As she picked her way through the woods, she heard someone singing.

Oh no. Lizzy.

Not today. There had to be a way to get to the house and plant her note on the front door without running into Lizzy.

Luna and Max were already sniffing frantically, their ears perking with each new round of singing, and the sound was coming closer. Why hadn't she left them in the pasture to patrol the fence line? Stupid. Maybe she should walk them home and return on her own. Or go out around the perimeter and come up to the other side of the house to get past Lizzy.

Taking a step backward, she prepared to turn in full retreat, but she forgot the boulder she'd avoided on her way in and tripped over it, falling arms first into leaf debris and pine cones.

"Ow! Shoot!" One pine cone lodged between her palm and the ground. Max and Luna both scurried over to her, sniffing and licking her to ensure she was all right. Max let out a loud woof as if to say, "You okay?"

She turned right side up and sat on her rear end, tallying up her wounds and fending off dog licks. "Thanks, guys. I'm good."

The dogs snapped to attention at something to her left and growled low in their throats. A rustling was coming—was it an animal or a person?

Then a head popped out from behind a tree. "Hey, Jan. I

thought I heard someone over here."

Lizzy.

"Hey, Lizzy." Jan forced as much resignation into her voice as she could manage. Perhaps she'd offend the girl and never hear from her again. *If only I were so lucky.*

Lizzy scooted around to her front and smiled down at her. "I thought we were each observing the boundary lines between our properties. I guess you changed your mind and came to visit?" Her smile looked so hopeful.

Jan glared up at the interloper and got up as gracefully as she could, ignoring the pine cones biting into her hands. "First, it isn't 'our' properties. It is my family's property and my best friend's family's property."

She brushed the leaves and dirt from her pants and hands. "And second, I wasn't coming to visit you. I was coming to leave a note for my best friend, who is moving back, by the way. So, you and your dad had better be packing up to leave." She donned a look harsh enough to wilt a newbie at cheer tryouts. She'd had enough of this person.

"Oh." The smile vanished. Lizzy scuffled her feet and clasped her hands together as if to keep them from shaking. "I'm glad your friend is coming back. I'll let my dad know."

"Do that." Jan stomped toward Renee's house with more determination than she'd ever felt.

The dogs loped behind her.

Then she pinned the note to the door, just as she used to when Renee lived there, though it had rarely been necessary since they'd been at each other's farms most days. She couldn't wait for those times to come again, to have a confidante back. She could picture her and Renee together again. Two peas in a pod, Mom used to call them.

Back home, she gave Max and Luna scratches under their chins and the command, "Hunt." They tore off in a beeline to the fence line for their patrol, racing each other. Obviously, the walk to Renee's house with her had been more relaxing for them than her, leaving them with pent-up energy to burn.

She entered the house. "I'm back."

"In the living room," Mom said.

Jan removed her shoes and placed them on the shoe rack, then joined Mom. This time, Mom's sewing was embroidery work. Some of the most amazing artwork Jan had seen was in her mother's neat, tight stitches. Pieces hung in various rooms of the house and adorned pillows, and even a locket Mom had made for her.

"What're you making?" When Jan plopped down beside Mom for a better look, Mom held it out for her to see. She'd painstakingly stitched an intricate blue bird onto a pillowcase. Jan traced the gossamer stitches, an aching for art class and a time when not everything revolved around survival tightening her chest. She swallowed down the ache. "It's beautiful. How do you make the wings look so real with just thread? What you can do amazes me."

Mom eased the fabric back toward herself and continued stitching. "It's a talent I honed when I was in bed sick for so long." She sighed as if remembering. "I'm not sure you can even imagine. But even after they knew I'd live, it took so long to recuperate enough to get around again. It gave me a lot of time sitting and lying around. I was glad to have my embroidery."

Jan kneaded her toes into the area rug, the clock ticking too loud again over her head as they sat in silence. She'd been in denial the whole time Mom was in the hospital, never once believing a sickness could undo her vital mother.

Tickkk-tickkk-tickkk! It seemed to be counting down to something.

She shivered, thinking of how the hospital only allowed one visitor in at the time. It was an improvement from the times when they permitted no visitors. Dad was Mom's designated one, and he would update them after each visit. Terror settled in because he wouldn't turn on Skype so she and Caleb could talk to Mom too. Now she understood they'd intubated Mom, and she was unable to speak.

Not going to think about Mom dying. Change of subject.

"I took the note over to Renee's house. Wouldn't you know it? I ran into Lizzy again." She rolled her eyes. "I swear the girl has a tracker on me."

With a chuckle, Mom elbowed her. "What happened?"

"I told her Renee was coming back, and they need to leave."

"No, sweetie." Mom shook her head, put her work down, and braced an arm on the canvas cushion behind Jan. "I mean, what happened to you?"

Uh-oh. A lecture was coming. "What are you talking about?"

"You used to have tons of friends. When you were small, if you couldn't have at least one friend with you, you turned your stuffed animals into friends. Remember?"

Jan chuckled. She and those stuffies had some especially fun parties. Bunny, Teddy, and the dogs would all have to dress up for tea if Renee or her other school friends weren't available.

"They all moved away, Mom. You know that."

As Mom's eyes got even more serious, Jan squirmed. Just what had she missed?

"Sweetie, you made friends with everyone. Why aren't you letting Lizzy into your life? She's not Jacob, and she needs someone to be her friend, just like you do."

Jan's heart pounded in her throat. "Are you crazy? How can you just forget what Jacob did to us?" She sprang from the comforting cushion and paced to the back of the couch. "We were lucky to get the truck back. Don't you remember how much trouble we were in? All because I trusted someone. It was *all my fault!*"

Mom tilted her head to the side, sighed, and patted the couch beside her. "Come over here. Deep breaths."

Jan flopped into her seat as Mom demonstrated slow inhalations and exhalations. It didn't help. Stiff as a board, Jan focused on the tension straining in her limbs.

"It's rarely a mistake to care for someone. We just forgot one vital lesson." Mom reached over to the side table for her well-worn Bible.

Surely, there wouldn't be a lesson in there about a truck thief. But then Mom always found a verse for every situation Jan had found herself in.

Mom handed over the Bible. "Read Matthew 10:16."

Jan fumbled through the pages to Matthew. At least it was the first book in the New Testament. It would disappoint Mom if she couldn't find the book and chapter after all the times they'd read Bible stories before bedtime when she was little.

She cleared her throat and read. " 'I am sending you out like sheep among wolves. Therefore, be as shrewd as snakes and as innocent as doves.' "

Mom slid her arm around Jan's waist and squeezed. "Jesus knew he wouldn't be around in his human form much longer. He was preparing his men to 'do battle' in a way. Sort of how we live now." She snugged Jan close, tipping their heads together until her dark hair tickled Jan's forehead. "This instruction tells his men they are to treat others gently and yet be smart enough to know when they might be in trouble. Does that make sense?"

"Exactly." She didn't understand why it wasn't obvious to her mom. "I wasn't shrewd like a snake. I was an idiot and brought a stranger into our home. I trusted him. And we all paid for it." She closed the book and handed it back. Point made.

"I would say we both learned our lesson there. But are you being innocent as a dove now with Lizzy?"

Jan cringed.

Shoot. Point made.

Chapter Fifteen

It was time to pick cucumbers. Jan eyed the long rows of plants. It would be an equally long day in the sun. Even though she'd started early, the heat would be on her soon. She placed her rolling garden bench between two rows, lay a bushel basket in front, and sat on the bench, breathing in the scent of warm earth and the mild, refreshing aroma of the cucumbers maturing on the vines.

The first plant on her left had grown huge with the supplemental nutrients from the composted chicken manure. Cleaning out the coop had been stinky and managing the composting process backbreaking, but these beautiful plants were worth the effort. She lifted the green leaves to inspect underneath.

This plant grew Kirby cucumbers. She plucked off three, the perfect size for pickling. Mom had already harvested dill weed and garlic from the greenhouse. The previous week, she'd worked out a good trade on market day for distilled vinegar. All they needed to do now was gather the fruit and process them.

Jan checked each plant for ripe fruit and then plucked the weeds that accumulated since her last visit. Caleb had to help Dad this morning, so Jan had plenty of time to think—and she needed time to ponder today. Mom's words from yesterday stuck in her head.

Was she being unfair to Lizzy, or was Mom being unrealistic? Times had changed. Mom was a soft touch.

Jan yanked a cucumber off the vine, and her thumb went right through it.

Yuck, rotten already.

It must have been one of the first ones on the vine.

She threw the spoiled fruit as far as she could and then wiped her hand on her jeans to clean off the goop. These pants were going in the wash the minute she got back.

She moved her bench to the next set of plants and sat back down. Before she could inspect the next plant, a loud bang jolted her.

A shotgun blast.

It had come from the front of the farm.

She sprang to her feet and sprinted toward the house. Who shot a gun? There shouldn't be anyone hunting today. Dad and Caleb were working on fences, and Mom never pulled a gun out.

Then she remembered. The trip wire. Had someone tripped it, setting off the early warning system?

Was their farm being invaded?

Her heart pounded with more than the exertion of running. She had to get back. Mom was alone, and Jan had left her gun behind this morning—stupid.

She met Dad and Caleb driving the golf cart and swung into a seat, too out of breath to speak.

"I'm dropping you at the house. Grab the shotgun out of the safe," Dad said to Caleb. "Tell your mother to stay in the house. Jan, stay with her until I figure out what's happening."

Seriously, could her heart pound even harder? Were they at

war now?

Dad stopped short at the house. Caleb jumped out and dashed to the front door. She was quick on his heels as Dad sped off toward the driveway.

Mom met them at the door, her eyes wide and wild, her hands reaching for Jan. "What happened? Is someone hurt?"

"We're fine, Mom." Caleb bypassed her in his sprint to the laundry room. Metal clicked as he opened the safe.

"Dad went to investigate, Mom." Jan eased out of Mom's grip. "He wants you to stay here until he figures out what's up." Twinning their hands, Jan tried to pull Mom toward the couch. With her eyes so wide and her breath so shallow, Mom needed to calm down. Did Caleb have to make such a ghastly racket loading the shotgun and slamming bullets into his pistol?

Her mom pushed her aside and hurried toward Caleb, but he met her coming out. "Mom, stay here. I'm going to back up Dad."

"You are *not* leaving this house with a loaded gun, young man." Mom blocked the front door.

Caleb's jaw set as he shoved the pistol into his holster. "I won't argue with you about this. Do you want Dad out there by himself?" He pushed toward the door, but Mom continued to block him.

Jan's heart thundered, and her stomach went all swooshy. Would she vomit with the tension?

"Give the guns to me." Mom held out her hand.

"No." Caleb sidestepped her. "I'm an adult now, and this is a man's business." He kissed her cheek as he pushed past.

The door slammed behind him.

When Mom broke down sobbing, Jan had to walk her over to the couch, rubbing her back in gentle circles. "It's okay," Jan crooned. "He knows how to shoot, and Dad won't let anything happen to him." After settling her mother, Jan hurried over to the door, yanked it open, and rushed out to the front porch as Caleb raced toward the traps. It was so hard to choose.

Should she go back and comfort Mom? Or follow her brother as backup?

Mom had moved off the couch. She was now on her knees, praying, head in her hands and elbows on the canvas couch cushion. She'd be fine in here alone.

As Jan rushed over to the gun safe, she started praying. "God, I only have time for a fast request here, but please keep us all safe." The safe was still open, so she hauled out the rifle she'd been practicing with. "And please don't let me have to shoot anyone."

Avoiding the front door so Mom wouldn't see the gun, Jan ran out the back.

Running with a rifle half her height was no easy feat. Caleb had just passed the stream trickling through a culvert under their driveway. That spurred her to move as quickly as the cumbersome gun would allow.

Wait a minute. They'd booby-trapped the driveway.

Caleb better remember the trip wire.

Stifling the temptation to holler out to him, she gritted her teeth. She didn't dare warn whoever set off the first trap of their arrival. With as much speed as she could muster, she tore up the driveway.

Before she could catch up with Caleb, Dad drove back toward them both. He waved his hands to get their attention and gave a stop motion. Half a football field's width behind Caleb, Jan froze in place, waiting for Dad's next instruction.

He skirted the edges of the second trip wire Caleb hadn't yet reached, then stopped and talked to her brother before starting toward her while Caleb walked up the driveway from where Dad had just been, avoiding the trip wire on his way.

As her dad pulled up to her, she burst out, "What happened? Who set it off?" She could barely get the words out as her heart slammed against her ribcage.

"It's okay. You can calm down." He grasped her shoulder. "It's Jacob. He's back, but he's not well. I sent Caleb up there to watch him. I need you to run back to your mom and tell her it was him."

Her heart sped up instead of calming. "No, Dad. You can't trust him. Maybe someone is with him again."

"I don't think so, kiddo. He's pretty sick." Dad squeezed her shoulder, then eased the gun away from her and tucked it onto the floor at his feet. "Tell you what. I'll run back up there and unhook the trip wire. Then you can stay with Caleb while I check around the house and look in on Mom. How does that sound?"

At her nod, he patted the seat beside him. "Hop in then."

After she joined him, he got out and went back to disconnect the trip wire. Once it was safe, she climbed out of the cart on wobbly legs.

"Don't touch him. We don't know what he's got," Dad said. "I'll bring back some masks and gloves. Until then, leave him where he's at."

She started walking to join Caleb as Dad drove back to the house. What tricks was Jacob up to this time? Even though Dad told her not to touch Jacob, she wanted to tie his hands. She might pull her belt off and do that.

As she crested the hill, Caleb was standing beside a lump of cloth. Once she got closer, the lump morphed into Jacob lying curled up on the ground with a blanket over him.

Caleb strode toward her. "He doesn't look so good."

She sprinted to his side and got a look at the boy's face. Sweat covered him. His skin was red under the filth, and he reeked. Hollows beneath his eyes and cheeks displayed his emaciation, and his slim form had shrunk since he'd been in their home.

She nudged the boy with her foot. "Jacob. You awake? Sit up."

Caleb put his hand on her arm. "Leave him be. You can see he's burning up."

"He could be faking." She bent to feel the boy's brow, but Caleb grabbed her arm and hauled her back up.

"Dad told me not to touch him. We don't know what he's got. It could be the variant."

Her stomach clenched, and she took a step back. "But he's not coughing. If he was sick with the variant, he'd be coughing, wouldn't he?"

"Not if he's almost gone. He hasn't moved since I've been here. So either he's passed out or on the way out." Hands on hips, Caleb surveyed the area as if searching for something.

"What are you looking for?"

"Just checking to be sure he's alone."

The truck grumbled up the hill. Dad parked beside them. "Caleb, I'm going to take the boy to Doc. You need to go back to your mom and keep an eye out to make sure this fellow isn't tricking us again. Before we leave, I'll reset both traps. Stay in the house until we're back."

Dad jumped from the truck with gloves and masks and handed a set to Jan as he put on his. She fit hers in place while Caleb started toward the house and Dad walked over to Jacob.

He bent down and pressed his gloved hand on the boy's

forehead. "Oh, that's not good. You're good and hot, son, aren't you?" He gently shook the small body. "Can you hear me, Jacob? Are you awake?"

Jacob's eyes opened, but they didn't seem to focus on anyone. "Mom?" He squirmed as if he wanted to sit up. "Thirsty. Mom?" He closed his eyes and relaxed again.

"It's okay. We'll get you some help." Dad scooped Jacob into his arms and carried him over to the back of the truck. "Pull down the tailgate, Jan."

After a quick wrestle with the worn-out handle, she finally got the rear door down.

"Climb up in there. I want you to ride in the back with him in case he wakes up. It's too risky to ride in the cab. The open air will cool him down and keep you from breathing in his germs. No telling what he's got."

Dad laid the boy on the tailgate once she'd scampered in. She tugged at the blanket under him to get him fully into the bed.

"It won't be the most comfortable ride in the world, but thump on the roof if you need anything en route." Dad ran back down the hill and reset both trip alarms, setting a bullet into the contraption that had already gone off. When he returned, he bobbed his head at her on the way past before getting into the cab.

It seemed like such a long ride to Doc's place. A few times, Jacob moaned. His eyes fluttered open and closed. "Mom... Can't see... Mom?"

She felt horrible. Who knew if his mother was even alive?

"Mom... thirsty." He sounded so weak.

"It's okay, Jacob. I'm right here." His face relaxed. Too bad she didn't have some water to cool him down.

Then Jacob went still, and his lips turned deathly pale.

"Jacob? Can you hear me, Jacob?"

No response.

She shook his arm. "Jacob."

No movement.

Was he even breathing?

Shoot! She pounded on the truck roof. "Dad, stop. Dad!"

The truck pulled over so suddenly that it threw her against the cab and the boy's body slid up to the cab as well.

"What's wrong?" Dad hollered as he jumped out.

"I don't think he's breathing." Tears streamed down her face, and she shook Jacob again.

With that shake, he gasped in a shallow breath, and color returned to his lips.

"Stay with us, son." Dad swung back into the truck. "Keep talking to him and hold on tight."

He hit the gas with enough force to send her sliding into the truck's bed, but toward the gate this time. Fortunately, Jacob slid with her, so they stayed side by side.

Jacob's mouth opened and closed like a guppy grabbing for food. After he did this a few times, she realized he was trying to talk, repeating over and over, "Mom."

Poor kid. He wanted comfort from someone who loved him. All she had been to him was someone who hated him. Did she hate him? Why would she hate him when she never knew him? They had only just met when he'd tricked them. Now she was all he had when he was trying to hang onto life, at an age when life hadn't really begun yet.

She put her cool hand on his fiery forehead. "I'm here, Jacob. I'll take care of you. Hold on."

Chapter Sixteen

Jan placed her gloved hand on Jacob's burning forehead, closed her eyes, and began praying. "God, I need some help here. I don't want Jacob to die. He's too young for that. He hasn't even lived yet."

The truck hit a pothole, and their bodies both lifted off the truck bed. When they landed, she found her hand on his shoulder. She left it there. "I don't think he'll ever be my bestie, God, but I don't want him gone anymore. I'm sorry about the mean things I thought. If you could heal him, I'll tell him I'm sorry myself."

Dad drove well over the speed limit, or so it felt. The potholes they hit tossed them into the air, and the corners he took sent them sliding into the sides. She continued her conversation with God in her head after they arrived and Dad scooped the boy's limp body off the tailgate.

Someone must have seen them coming, because the door opened, and they dashed into the waiting room. The young woman at the front desk popped out of her chair and led them to an open exam room. "Get rid of the blanket while I grab Doc," she said, then ran back out.

In a sterile environment, the filth of Jacob's body was even more evident, and the smell was horrendous. More than dirt covered his small face, and gunk trailed from his nose, forming globs in his dark hair—hadn't it been red before? Dad lifted him from the blanket, and Jan heaved it out from under him. With the only trash can in the room being too small, she scurried out through the lobby and tossed the blanket into the truck bed.

Then she hustled back via the same route to help however she could. When she entered the room again, Doc and another woman were examining the boy while Dad stood by the door. She joined him, continuing in her silent plea.

"He's not yours, Steve. How do you know the boy?" Doc asked. "How long has he been sick?"

"Sorry, Doc. I don't know." Dad shoved his hands in his pockets. "Let's say we met a while back and he showed up on the farm today in this shape."

The assistant clamped a glass thermometer under Jacob's armpit while Doc pulled open one of his eyelids and shined a penlight into it. Then Doc used his stethoscope to listen to Jacob's chest while the nurse checked the thermometer. "Pulse 120. Temperature 102.3."

"Is he going to be okay?" Jan shoved her twitchy hands behind her and shifted from foot to foot, barely able to stand not knowing what to do.

Doc's face softened. "He's malnourished and dehydrated. I think he's got a virus. He's not coughing, and his lungs are clear—so that's in his favor."

The nurse peeled Jacob's shirt off. White skin practically glowed underneath in contrast to the grubby hands and face. After tossing it in the trash can, the nurse eyed Jan. "I need to take the rest of his clothes off. You might want to wait in the lobby."

Her face burning, Jan slogged out of the room and shuffled

to the waiting room. However, her muscles kept twitching. Sitting still in the chair *hurt*—actually hurt.

Staying there was no use, so she left the building and paced around the truck, waiting for Dad to bring news.

Still, it seemed like an eternity before he joined her. When he stepped out the door, she popped up off the truck tailgate like a jack-in-a-box. His face looked tired, but not as concerned as when they'd arrived. He removed his mask and gloves.

"Come over here for a minute, kiddo." When she walked over, he snuggled her into a tight hug. "We have to cherish every day we have each other—you know that."

She nodded, her face rubbing up and down on his sweat-sodden T-shirt. When he released her, a threatening tear slipped down her cheek, and her heart thudded in her throat. "Is he going to be okay?"

"I think so." His tired eyes turned toward the ground. "Doc gave him fluids, and they're cleaning him up now. He's awake—a good sign—and thirsty as all get out."

Oh, thank you, God. Thank you. She surged forward to hug him tight.

"They're also giving him peanut butter, if you can believe that." He let out a laugh as he patted her back and strode toward the truck.

"Peanut butter?"

"Doc says it was a trick he used when he was young and went on mission trips to poor countries." Dad jumped up on the tailgate and patted the seat for her to join him. "Says peanut butter was a quick way to help malnourished kids back then, so he's doing the same for our boy."

Our boy? That sounded odd.

She crawled onto the tailgate with Dad giving her a good tug up. Situated, she tucked flyaway red hair behind her ears and slid off her mask and gloves as well. "What are we going to do now?"

"We're going to wait here for a while longer. Doc said he doesn't have any place to keep him overnight. So, after they've filled him with fluids, we'll take him home with us." He cocked his head to one side and eyed her.

Seriously? Take Jacob back home?

"But he's sick. We can't have him around Mom. What are we going to do with him?"

"We'll keep them apart." Dad draped an arm around her and jostled her close. "You should take care of him till he's strong enough to take care of himself again. Can you do that?"

"Yes, sir." She threaded her arm around his back and squeezed with all her might. "I can."

They waited until it was almost dark for Doc to release the patient. Dad carried Jacob back to the truck and tucked him into the back seat, buckling him into place.

Jacob eyed her wearily, but couldn't maintain eye contact and looked down into his lap. Doc had put a set of hospital scrubs on the boy. The shirt hung below his knees, but they'd rolled the legs and sleeves to expose his hands and feet.

"You're coming back to the farm with us," Dad said. "Just rest for the ride home, and we'll get you situated for the night. It'll be okay, son."

Jacob relaxed into the corner of the seat and closed his eyes. His head drooped into sleep within minutes. He slept the rest of the way home and through the night in the spare bedroom.

Worried about him, Jan only got snippets of rest between checking on him. His past deception hovered in her brain, and she couldn't quite trust that he was here alone, even though

Max and Luna hadn't alerted on anything.

She'd also passed Dad in the upstairs hallway a few times during the night. It appeared they were taking turns checking on the boy without having planned it. Several times, she heard Jacob calling for his mom. The poor guy seemed so alone and, in his weakened state, so small. Her heart ached to give him to his mother for the hugs any sick kid needed.

As the sun rose, she gave up any further attempts at sleep, dressed in jeans and a T-shirt, and padded out to the kitchen. Dad fried potatoes in a pan as Mom, on a stool at the counter, worked on her embroidery project.

"Morning, sunshine." Dad flipped potatoes without looking her way. "Our patient's still asleep."

She should have checked on him herself, but her brain must have still been fuzzy. "I'll check on him again and take more water."

"Good idea. I helped him drink most of it last night. You'll have to help him again, though."

"Why don't you sit and rest a spell." Mom rose. "I can check on him for you."

"No way!" Jan reversed her trajectory of sitting on a stool and popped over to snag a glass out of the cabinet.

"I agree with Jan." Dad shook the spatula Mom's way, dropping a bit of grease on the hardwood floor. "Doc said the boy probably isn't contagious, just caught a virus because of his weakened state. But you are *not* to go anywhere near that boy until he's well enough to come out—you hear me? I don't need two sick patients at once."

Mom glared as she sank back onto the stool and picked up her work. "Why do I have to keep reiterating this? *I am. Not. An invalid.*"

Jan knew better than to respond to this outburst. Best to leave it to Dad. She filled the water glass, snagged a jar of homemade peanut butter, and took them, along with a spoon, to Jacob's room. At the door, she knocked and slid it open to peek inside. "Jacob? You awake?"

He stared at her from the bed and tried to sit up, but he only made it to his elbows before collapsing. Then he pulled the covers over his head as if he could hide from her.

"Yeah, you probably don't feel like getting up, huh?"

The smell of unwashed child assaulted her nose as she drew closer to the bed. The nurse had cleaned his arms up enough to insert the IV safely the day before but hadn't had time to attempt to bathe Jacob. He wasn't strong enough to sit up, but he needed a bath. First things first, though.

"I brought you more water and some peanut butter." She nudged the empty glass on the bedside table. "Doc said you should eat it here and there until your stomach adjusts to food again. If you keep it down, Mom will make you some soup. And you don't want to miss out on Mom's beef vegetable soup. Believe me."

He remained under the covers, but his stomach gurgled.

"I won't bite you. Come on out." She set the glass, spoon, and jar on the bedside table, then tugged on the blanket. He held on, trying to remain in his cocoon. But being stronger, she wrestled the blankets down. As his head popped into view, he shut his eyes.

What was with the kid? Sure, he was undersized, but what was he? *Five?* Like closing his eyes would make her disappear.

She rolled her eyes. "Jacob. Really? I need to get you sitting up so you can drink more water and eat some peanut butter."

No response except his eyes squeezed shut even tighter and

his mouth scrunched up as if he was steeling himself to avoid being force-fed.

"If you don't let me help you, I'll just send in Caleb or Dad. So who do you want to deal with—them or me?" She stood with hands on hips, eyes glaring.

His eyelids popped back open. "'K."

She'd have to remember that threat for the future. "Try to sit up again. I'll help this time."

When he did as instructed, she moved him into a sitting position with pillows piled behind him. She sat on the edge of the bed and brought the glass to his lips. He held it along with her, his hands shaking as he gulped. After consuming half of it, he released it and closed his eyes as if in relief.

Next, she opened the jar of peanut butter and scooped a dollop on the spoon. Holding it up to his mouth, she said, "Try to eat a little at a time for now. The last thing we want is for it to come back up again."

At first, he nibbled at the spoon's edges but soon consumed it. Once he'd licked it clean, she put the lid back on the jar.

"That's it for now. Do you want to stay sitting up? Or do you want to lie back down again?"

He let out a tremendous sigh and whispered, "I have to use the bathroom."

Ugh, oh! She hadn't thought of that. He wouldn't be able to make it into the bathroom by himself, and she wasn't going to help him with the necessities of life.

"Wait here. I'll be right back."

As she dashed out, she chuckled. How silly she must have sounded. Like he could jump out of the bed and run away.

Dad was spooning the potatoes into a serving bowl when she popped into the room.

"We've got a problem in Paradise, Dad."

He dropped the pan on the stove, alert to an emergency. "What's wrong?"

"Sorry, nothing major. He's fine. He just has to go to the bathroom."

He relaxed and laughed. "Ah, men's work."

"Yes, please."

"I'll let you scramble the eggs while I take care of business then." Off he went, and Jan cracked eggs into a bowl to whisk.

"How's he doing?" Mom asked.

"Looks a lot better than he did yesterday, but weak." She took the potato pan, put some lard into it, and turned on the stove. "We have another problem, though, after Dad takes him to the bathroom. He stinks... bad."

"Well, I guess the men of the house are going to get a lesson in mothering then, aren't they?" Mom chuckled.

Jan smiled at the thought of big, tough Caleb bathing the boy. Time to put the eggs on to cook.

Chapter Seventeen

In the three days since Jacob had moved into the spare bedroom, he looked like a new kid. His hair, now clean, looked red again, his eyes no longer hollow, and he smelled like a normal human, not a backed-up septic tank. Having already brought him his breakfast, Jan now sat with the family, enjoying their morning meal.

"We can safely assume Jacob is not contagious." Dad eyed Mom. "No fever, sitting up fine and walking to the bathroom and back on his own. Shall we invite him to join us for dinner?"

"You already know what I think. Let me go in and get his sheets changed." Mom dropped her fork, the bite of food uneaten. "I'm sure he'd like to come out right now."

"I can change the sheets." Jan stood, ready to end his quarantine.

But Mom waved her back down. "Let him finish his breakfast in peace before he has to face all of us at once. We need to figure out what to do with him since he's getting better."

"I'll go talk to the police today." Dad shoveled up a forkful of eggs. "They'll want to do some sort of investigation to find his next of kin. He hasn't been willing to talk to me at all, much less discuss his current family situation."

Jacob said little to anyone. Jan heard him crying some nights and even calling for his mother in his dreams. She couldn't imagine how alone he must feel, stuck in a house he'd helped steal from. They'd all tried to get him to open up, but he was stubbornly silent other than monosyllable responses.

After breakfast, she cleaned the kitchen while Mom changed Jacob's sheets. Mom's voice drifted downstairs in soft conversation, but no audible responses followed. He had a subdued voice, so maybe Jan just couldn't hear his responses.

Mom passed through the kitchen to the laundry room with an armful of bedding. "I'm wondering if that boy even knows how to speak at this point. He wouldn't say a word to me. Why don't you try again?"

Jan started the dishwasher as Mom moved into the laundry room, humming. After drying her hands, Jan went up to check on him. He sat in the bed with a book. His shirt was one of Caleb's old ones, and he'd rolled the sleeves up so many times they resembled small inner tubes. His bony wrists were obvious as he shoved a sleeve up and flipped a page.

"Dad says you can leave the room now. I'll bet you'll be glad to be out of here, huh?"

He looked at her, then back down at the book.

"Today, Dad will go into town to talk to the police."

"No!" Jacob's eyes went wide. "I won't steal again. I promise. I didn't want to do it." He balled himself up with his knees to his chest and rocked front and back.

"Hey, calm down. I didn't get to finish." She moved over to touch his arm, but he pulled away and scurried to the opposite side of the bed.

"Chill, dude." She backed away to allow him space. "Dad is just getting the police to look for your family. He's not turning you in."

He stopped rocking, his eyes wide. Then he lowered his head onto his arms and sobbed so suddenly it must have been waiting to come out.

Her stomach flipped, queasy at seeing him so distraught. "What is it? I said he's not turning you in. You won't go to jail."

Too bad she couldn't rub his back or something to comfort him, but he resisted everything she'd tried. Not wanting to make it worse, she hated this helpless feeling.

"Talk to me, buddy. I don't know what's wrong."

His shoulders continued to shake, his head still buried against his knees, so she sat there, inept. Mom would know what to do.

Jan rose, and the boy shifted at her movement, eyes red and cheeks soggy. He wiped his snotty nose on his shirt sleeve. *Yuck.*

"They won't find anyone."

Sitting back down, she met his gaze. "What do you mean? Is your family not from here?"

"Dad is dead." He used the opposite sleeve to wipe his eyes dry. "Mom left and never came back."

A lump formed in her throat. "Was that your dad they found in the truck?"

"No. My uncle." He shifted his whole body away from her. "Mom's brother. He didn't get along with my dad, but he was the only family I had left. Now I don't have him either."

What do you say to a kid who lost his entire family? Mom really needed to get in here. Jan could cheer someone on like nobody's business, but cheering them up? That was something else entirely.

"I'm going to get Mom." She smiled. "She'll know what to do."

His head lowered back down to rest on his arms, still wrapped around his knees. At least he didn't hide his eyes. He just watched her, resigned.

"Dad died last year from the variant. Then Mom left me with my uncle." His eyes were vacant as if he was telling himself what happened, instead of sharing his story. "Uncle Mike lived with us because he didn't have a job. Dad always complained about that, said Uncle Mike would end up in prison someday. He told me to keep my distance from him." A choked laugh escaped. "That didn't work out so well."

She fidgeted. Why wasn't Mom here to hear his story? "Is that how you ended up being a thief? Did your uncle talk you into it?"

A fresh tear slid down his cheek. "Mom would be mad if she knew. 'Thou shall not steal.' She taught me the commandments from the Bible. You know about those?"

"I do. Why did you do it if you knew it was wrong?" Confusion churned in her mind. His mother had taught him right from wrong and guilt filled his eyes.

"Uncle Mike said I had to pay my way. Said it wasn't fair for him to be stuck taking care of me. Now he's dead too. I guess I deserve to be alone." Jacob hid his eyes in his arms once more. "I was bad."

His confession came out in barely a whisper—the poor kid.

"That's all over." She braved touching his shoulder. "You don't have to do that now."

He tensed under her touch. Then his shoulders sagged and he shivered as he cried.

He was just a kid. She couldn't imagine losing Mom, Dad, and Caleb. What would she do without them? Would she turn to stealing as well? If she were honest with herself, she'd do whatever she had to do to survive.

"Rest, buddy. I'll make sure you're okay."

He scooted underneath the covers, and she snugged them up over him. Before going to find her mom, she went to the bathroom and gathered some handkerchiefs. Then she took them back and laid them on the bedside table, handing one to Jacob to wipe his nose. He accepted it and closed his eyes.

«»

When Dad came home, he wasn't alone. Officer Bradley followed him into the house. Jan sat with her mother on the couch, discussing Jacob's story, wondering what the police would do.

Officer Bradley introduced himself to Mom, nodding at Jan as he did. "I wanted to interview the boy."

Jan surged to her feet, propelled by a sudden urge to protect the boy. "You can't. He's sleeping."

Dad shot her a puzzled look. "We can wake him up, kiddo. The officer has important questions for him. We need to find his family."

"He doesn't have any. He told me." She moved to stand between the policeman and the stairwell as if she could bar him from Jacob's room with her body.

The officer raised his eyebrows. "Little lady, I need to ask him questions. I know how to get answers out of kids. Leave the investigating to me."

Little lady?

Her face burned. If her parents hadn't taught her better, she'd have stomped on his foot and kicked his shin with every ounce of strength she had. But she knew to respect authority— even when they didn't respect her.

Well, if Jacob was going to be interrogated, he wouldn't be

alone. She stomped upstairs to the bedroom and preceded the men into the room. Jacob rolled over and opened his eyes. As he spotted the police officer, he bolted up, eyes wide.

"It's okay, buddy," she said. "He's only here to ask you questions. I'm not leaving you alone, though." She planted herself beside him on the bed, putting her arm around him. As he cowered into her side as if she was a refuge, she stared at the officer and hardened her face, prepared for battle.

The officer asked no questions about the stolen truck or the crimes Jacob and his uncle might have committed, but he tossed questions at Jacob in rapid-fire as though trying to catch him in a lie. Jacob's answers never changed.

After the officer finished, he stepped out of the room and took Dad with him. She stayed with Jacob, rubbing his shoulder. She wasn't sure why she felt a need to protect the kid.

"See?" She jostled him like a little brother. "Nothing to worry about. He's gone, and you're still here safe."

He remained silent for a couple of beats. "I'm tired. Can I sleep now?"

"Of course." She got up and covered him up as he slid back under the blankets. "I'll wake you for dinner if you aren't up before then."

She walked out, closing the door behind her, and headed to the quiet discussion in the kitchen. Officer Bradley was speaking to Mom and Dad when she walked in.

"... so we don't have any social services available. All I can do is take him into the station to keep him safe until I can find a home to place him in."

She'd promised him. He wouldn't understand. "What? No! You can't put him in jail."

"Little lady, we don't have any place to put him tonight."

Fiery heat rose in her throat, threatening to choke her. What she wanted to say seared the tip of her tongue, but her mother's face told her to swallow it.

"Can't he stay here?" Mom's calm voice soothed Jan's rough edges. "We have the room. If family turns up, you'll know where he is."

Jan leveled her best pleading expression on Dad, who nodded. "The boy is safer here than in a place full of criminals."

"It wouldn't be a bad idea for him to stay here until I can get some calls in to Columbus. They still have some social services, though I doubt they'd place the boy right away as strained as they are."

"It's settled then. He'll be here if you ever find some family to claim him." Mom smiled at the officer.

So, that was it. For the time being, they had another family member. She wondered what that was going to be like—and if he was truly alone in the world.

How could a mother abandon her child as Jacob's mother had done?

Chapter Eighteen

Over the next few days, Jacob almost melted into the furniture, unseen and silent. The most she heard from him was at night when he called out for his mother while asleep. Mom responded to his cries, comforting him just as she had with Jan's nightmares as a child.

"You feel up to picking cucumbers with me today, Jacob?" Jan asked. He'd been outside to see the calves with Caleb yesterday. But the men were busy today, taking down a tree before it fell on the fences. That meant he had no plans for the day. He stared out the windows, fidgeting with the rolled-up sleeves on the sweatshirt Caleb had loaned him.

Mom, who'd set up her sewing machine in the dining room and was cutting down a pair of old jeans to fit Jacob, gave a firm nod. "Sounds like a good idea. You can wear my garden boots, Jacob. Just triple up on the socks so they don't fall off."

He scuffled his feet and wiggled his toes. Jan's socks were too big for him, but he'd stretched them up over the sweatpants to his lower calf to keep from tripping over the pant legs.

"Yes, ma'am." After a dash to his room for more socks, he followed Jan to the laundry room and the line of work boots.

Mom's garden boots, with yellow daisies printed all over them, waited on the boot rack. Jan pointed them out and grinned at his resigned look. "I know. I'm not a fan of flowers on boots either."

He plopped down on the floor and pulled on the extra socks, then slid on the offending footwear, which had to be better than trekking around just in his socks as he'd been when she chased him.

"I'm sure we can find you some boots on auction day. I know a lady who sells used clothes," Jan said.

A smile spread across his lips.

"Dad and Caleb had to take the truck." She grabbed keys off the key rack and handed them to him. "So you get to drive the golf cart out to the garden."

His eyes grew wide as he took the fob from her. "I don't know how, though."

"Shoot, it's easy. It's nothing like an actual car. You can take it slow until you've got the hang of it." Smiling at him, she opened the door and ushered him out.

"Really?" He stood frozen in front of the cart.

As she gathered the basket, the rolling stool, and two sets of gloves, he climbed into the driver's seat and put the key in the ignition.

"Carts are easy." She joined him in the front seat. "All you have to do is turn the key to the On position and then push the gas pedal."

He stared at the pedals.

"The vertical one on the right is the accelerator—that makes it move forward." She pointed to the correct one. "The horizontal pedal next to it is the brake—that'll stop you."

He turned the key in the ignition, his scrawny shoulders tense as his tongue snaked through his lips.

She stifled the urge to laugh. Had she looked so in awe when

Caleb taught her? "You got it, Squirt." The name felt right. They had a new squirt in the family. "Press down the gas pedal."

He stomped it hard, and the cart lurched forward. The sudden movement caused him to take his foot back off the pedal, and they slowed to a stop. Alternating between stomping and releasing, they jerked forward a few hundred yards.

If he didn't get this figured out soon, she'd get whiplash.

"Push it slow and steady and then let go of it when you want to slow down." Could you get whiplash from a golf cart ride?

When he worked the pedals with more finesse, the cart moved farther toward the garden, and the ride became smoother. Halfway to their destination, a huge grin spread over his face, triumphant with his new knowledge.

At the garden plot, she pointed to the side ready to be harvested. "Park down there at the end."

After he stopped and switched off the cart, she got out, and he followed. She handed him a set of gloves and the empty basket. Then she donned her gloves and pulled out the stool.

"I'm afraid I've only got one stool. Why don't you sit and pick, and I'll pull the basket along in front of us?"

As he sat on the stool she'd planted in the path between the two rows, she bent, lifted the leaves on the first plant, and picked two perfectly sized cucumbers. She held them out for him to see. "These are the right size for pickling. Do you like pickles?"

He shrugged.

"Have you tried pickles?"

Another shrug.

Just then, a commotion broke out on the property's far side. Max and Luna had found something and were carrying on. It was probably Lizzy again. Shouldn't she have learned by now?

Jacob's brow furrowed as he twisted toward the barking. "What are they barking at?"

"Most likely our annoying neighbors." Jan continued pulling cucumbers from the plants. "Or rather the people squatting on our neighbors' land."

His eyebrows rose upward.

She huffed out a breath. "They shouldn't be there. My best friend used to live there, and these people just moved onto their land with their RV. It's not a nice thing to do."

"That's bad," he said.

The dogs had stopped barking.

Then the dinner bell clamored.

"Uh-oh." Jan stood. "Something's up. Let's go."

She dashed back to the cart with him close behind. Before he could claim the spot, she jumped into the driver's seat and started the ignition while he climbed in beside her. The truck had already returned home. Six people stood beside it. Her throat felt tight, and her mouth went dry. Who was at the house?

Six people. Easy enough to recognize Mom, Dad, and Caleb just from the clothes they'd been wearing this morning. So who were the other man and two women? No, not two women. A woman and a teenager.

Renee!

Jan's heart leaped. Was it really her best friend?

Yes!

And the man standing beside her father was Mr. Boswell. They were back.

The cart was no longer moving fast enough for her, and the last 200 yards to the house felt like a snail's pace. At fifty yards out, she stopped the cart, jumped out, and ran straight into her best friend's outstretched arms.

Squeals were all she could manage as tears flowed down her face. Finally, after what felt like an eternity, they were back together. Double trouble, united again.

As soon as she could manage it, she grabbed Renee, and they escaped to her bedroom for some catch-up time.

"I've missed you so much. You have no idea." She plopped down on the bed and crossed her legs, face flushed. She leaned against the daybed's metal side rail. "Tell me *everything*."

Renee jumped on the end of the bed, crossed her legs, and stuck her pointer finger in the air. "First, Columbus was horrible. Dad could find work only once in a while. We all pitched in when we could find odd jobs, but it stunk."

She shot up her middle finger to join the first. "Second, we were staying with Dad's family, and it was sooo crowded. And just so you know, my cousin is creepy."

Her ring finger jutted up. "Third, I missed you horribly. I'm so glad to be back."

Jan bounced. *Finally. Girl time.* Then another thought hit her. "What did your dad do about the squatters?"

"You mean Lizzy and her dad? Aren't they great?"

Jan's spine stiffened, and she gawked at her friend. Seriously, had an alien taken over her body? After a moment's pause, she realized her mouth was open like a bass caught on a jig. "Great? Have you actually met Lizzy?"

Renee's eyes narrowed. "Well, of course, I have. Why do you say it like that? She's so sweet. And her dad has been taking care of the place. They'll be staying for a while. Won't it be great to have another girl around? We should plan a sleepover!"

Jan's eyebrows shot up. *She's lost her mind.* "Are we talking about the same girl? The girl I know is so annoying. She talks so fast you can barely keep up, and she never stops yapping."

The furrow on Renee's face deepened. "Annoying? She's great! What's going on between you two? She said you were kind of quiet. And that's so not true."

"You need to hear the entire story." Jan nestled in and told her BFF all about how she met Jacob. Renee gasped at the theft, and then her eyes grew red and watery at the death of Jacob's uncle. Next, Jan moved on to the story of the dogs.

Renee nodded. "Yes, we met them. They're good at their jobs."

Jan ended her story with the appearance of the interlopers. "So, you see why you can't just trust these people. They may seem all friendly, but the next thing you know, they're walking off with your valuables."

Renee swooshed her sheet of blond hair over her shoulders. "So, just because someone else tricked you, everyone is a suspect?"

Jan flapped her hands up in the air. "Of course not. But can't you see how they shouldn't just be moving onto someone else's land without permission?"

"It's not like they had anyone to ask, did they? And have you tried to get to know Lizzy? I've only known her for a few hours, and I can't wait to spend more time with her. It's hard to find good friends these days, you know."

That settled it. Renee had lost her mind. "So, one meeting and you trust her?" Jan physically pulled back from her friend as if proximity would leach stupidity onto herself.

"Have you even tried to get to know her before judging her?" Renee's eyes narrowed again, and she crossed her arms over her chest.

Uh-oh. This was a familiar move. *Better tread carefully if you don't want a fight.* Renee always stood up for the underdog. Was it possible Jan had been too quick to judge? Or was Renee too naïve?

"I don't want to fight. Can we change the subject?" Jan used her best sad-puppy-dog eyes. But Renee's arms remained crossed, so Jan jutted out her lower lip and tilted her head downward. When there was still no reaction, she turned her lips up in a smile.

That was the ticket. Her best friend smiled and then blew out a chuckle. "All right. Let's talk about something else for now. But this discussion isn't over, just paused."

"Agreed." Best to wait until her friend got a better sense of reality where it was every man for himself. Then she'd be ready to pick up the pieces of her friend's broken heart over the betrayal Lizzy was sure to bring.

A rap on the door caught their attention, and Caleb yelled from the other side, "Dinner."

They joined the family in the dining room. Someone had added back the table extensions to fit eight people around it and brought in the extra metal chairs from the patio. Candelabra lights glowed on the rustic chandelier above it, creating a homey atmosphere. Memories of Thanksgiving meals came to her mind as she sat between her BFF and her brother. However, now they had a newcomer. Jacob sat opposite Caleb.

As they enjoyed the turkey dinner, Jan teased Caleb over the shotgun pellet in her slice of the bird. "Almost broke a tooth on that one." She held it up for all to see, then winked at Renee. "No one warned Jacob to chew cautiously when it's a turkey Caleb shoots and cleans."

"Oh man. I thought I'd gotten them all. Sorry," Caleb said.

"Still the tastiest bird I've had in a while," Mr. Boswell said. "All kidding aside, though, we need to discuss our plan of action." He braced both forearms on the table and faced Dad as if this was a continuation of a conversation dinner had interrupted.

"Probably not the best dinner conversation, honey." Mrs. Boswell slid her hand over to his arm.

"It's the perfect time. Everyone is here. There's no reason to hide reality from our children." He stared at Renee, sitting opposite him. "They aren't infants. It's time they realized how dangerous our world has become."

Jan studied her father to gauge how worried she should be. His face seemed frozen as if to mask any expression leaking out. Across from him, Mom's cheeks had pinked.

Something was up. Maybe Jan should have spent a little time with the adults before dinner. One could miss important information when they left adults alone for too long.

"Perhaps after we finish eating?" Mom's eyes pled with Mr. Boswell.

"I'm good," Jan said. "Don't know that I can risk any more dental accidents on this turkey, anyway."

She ribbed her brother with her elbow in the hopes he'd join in the levity and help to lighten the mood. If she played it right, they'd explain what was going on.

"Yeah, I'm good too," Caleb said. "What's going on?"

Whew, he got the message.

Exhaling a heavy breath, Dad set down his fork, swallowed his last mouthful of food, and began. "Mr. Boswell saw a gang of thugs in Waverly Hall on his way from Columbus. They avoided the gang, but they're headed our way."

"It's a dangerous group of both men and women." Mr.

Boswell crossed his arms over his chest and rocked back in his chair, the metal legs squeaking against the hardwood floor as they scooted off the area rug. "They stole horses and act like they're living back in the Wild West. But they're definitely men in black hats. We need to be ready when they get here because, I assure you, they are coming. As soon as they bleed that town dry, they'll move on. Maybe even before then."

Jan's stomach churned at the thought of men riding up their driveway, intent on taking whatever they could. Then she remembered the traps.

"We're ready. Right, Dad?" Confident in her father's contraptions, she presented the thumbs-up signal at her father.

"Probably not as much as we should be, kiddo." Dad peered down the table at Mom, whose eyes were filling at the mention of conflict. "Probably not as much as we should be."

Chapter Nineteen

They sat at the table for another hour, discussing strategies for keeping their properties safe.

"It sounds like you're in fairly good shape, Steve," Mr. Boswell said. "The traps protect the front drive. Dogs running the perimeter are great as well, but they can't protect the entire one hundred acres at once."

Dad rubbed his stubbled chin. "I'm more worried about your property than ours at this point. We can set some traps, but you're too exposed out there. The Tilbrooks' RV is especially vulnerable."

Jan slid her hand into Renee's and squeezed. Her bestie's face had gone too pale.

Jacob cleared his throat. "Excuse me."

He so rarely spoke, everyone's attention focused on him. That, combined with the sudden silence, appeared to unnerve him. He dropped his gaze to the table and fidgeted with his fork as if hoping more food would appear on his plate as he spoke.

"I know you have extra rooms in this house. My uncle always told me there's strength in numbers." He tried to make eye contact with Dad but blinked each time he connected as if it was painful. "You could all stay on this farm together. You could have the Tilbrooks move their RV here too. Then you'd have more people to watch the fence lines with Max and Luna."

After the mention of the dogs, he snapped his mouth shut as if they'd scolded him and returned his gaze to his empty plate.

With a wide grin, Dad clamped a hand on Jacob's shoulder. "Good idea, Jacob. I don't know why I didn't think of it first."

"We couldn't impose like that." Mrs. Boswell spoke up. "It wouldn't be easy to have so many people in one home."

"Actually," Mom said, "it's not a bad idea. We have plenty of space, and the walk-in attic was never even finished over the garage. That area could accommodate two bedrooms." Her smile grew. "We could turn it into a temporary space until we figure out something more permanent."

"Renee can stay in my room with me." Jan looped her arm through her bestie's. "It would be like a long sleepover."

"Jacob can bunk with me." Caleb got in on the action as well. "Then you could use the spare bedroom too."

"If you don't think it's too much"—Mr. Boswell rubbed his hands together as if getting ready to tackle a colossal task—"we can help on the farm to earn our keep."

Grins formed as they made plans to move the Boswells in. Jacob smiled at Jan from across the table. She winked in response.

《》

On moving day, everyone put in sweat equity to transport the most important Boswell possessions along with their necessary items. The Tilbrooks agreed to move their RV over to the farm.

Jan managed to avoid Lizzy during the move, but there was no avoiding the interloper during supper. The dining room was now at full capacity with ten people sitting at the table. Dad had put both extensions in, and the spare chairs now fulfilled their original purpose.

The scents of cornbread and savory beef stew had been the dinner bell to bring everyone in. The stew was one of her favorite meals.

She had to speak a little louder than usual for Renee to hear, as three different conversations were going on. Lizzy also kept butting in.

"I can't believe I'm living on a farm now." Lizzy mashed her cornbread into her stew. "Will my clothes stink of cow patties?"

Jan sighed. "Only if you decide to roll in one."

What an idiot. Renee's elbow jabbed Jan in the side at an angle no one would have noticed except for her sore ribs.

"Yuck. That's disgusting, but *this* is sooo good! I haven't had anything this tasty in, well, I can't remember when we had something this good. How about you, Dad?" Lizzy bounced a little. With her eyes bright, she sat on the edge of her chair as if prepared to spring up at any moment. "And the hot shower, you can't imagine how good that felt! It's like living in a palace here. Can I help with chores tomorrow? I've never fed a cow before."

"I'm glad you asked, Lizzy." Dad jumped into the conversation with a voice that commanded the attention of all before he connected eye to eye with each person. "We're going to have to set up work schedules. This farm can support ten people. Of that, I have no doubt. But we'll have to work as a team to make it happen."

"We'll do whatever is needed, of course."

At Mr. Boswell's words, all the guests nodded like bobblehead dolls.

«»

Dad made one list of outside chores and another for inside

tasks. Having other people in the garden with her, harvesting, weeding, and watering to keep the produce coming, felt good. Today, they worked as a team to harvest the cucumbers for canning.

Jan oversaw the transportation of full baskets to the house and empty baskets to the pickers while Lizzy, Jacob, and Renee harvested the fruits and weeded as they traversed the rows. Earlier, Jan had dropped off a basket with the ladies in the kitchen. Mrs. Boswell had been washing and slicing the soon-to-be pickles while Mom prepared the jars and brine. The kitchen smelled of vinegar and pickling spices, one of Jan's favorites.

She'd refilled the water bottles and placed them in the back of the golf cart for the picking team. The day's heat was setting in, and no way would she deal with heat exhaustion again. So they'd all be knocking off on the picking soon and heading to the house to help with the processing.

She'd thought planning four rows of pickling cucumbers had been too much during the planting phase. But Mom had wanted plenty to sell, saying they'd been the only vendor to have them last year and God would provide a way to get them all harvested and processed.

Now, as Jan drove the cart out to the field, she could see how God had answered Mom's prayers. Mom never lost faith. Perhaps it was time Jan followed in her mother's steps and spent more time praying about the important things.

She pulled up to the garden and hollered, "I've got your water bottles. Let's take a break."

Lizzy, Renee, and Jacob all stood, faces beet red, and made their way to the cart. Once they arrived, each grabbed a bottle and chugged the water.

"I had no idea how hard farming was." Lizzy swiped at her sweaty brow. "I may want to do something besides farming when I'm out on my own."

Renee coughed as she drank from her bottle and ended up spewing water instead of swallowing it. After she finished hacking, she laughed. "How did you think food got to people's tables before someone invented all the machines to pick vegetables?"

Lizzy shrugged. "I never thought about it. Why would I have to? We just bought our food."

Jan laughed now too. "And how's that been working out for you lately?"

Jacob placed his empty bottle back in the cart. "My uncle taught me how to steal from people's gardens to eat. It's a lot nicer to help pick, though, instead of taking what isn't yours."

No one said anything. Jan didn't know how to respond. She'd been so angry at him after he helped his uncle steal their truck.

"Let's get packed up and head back to the house," she said. "Dad's going over our plans this afternoon for who does what if we're attacked."

The others went sullen. Each walked back to their respective rows, gathered their baskets, and loaded up the golf cart. She drove them to the house and helped cart baskets into the kitchen.

"Hold up, guys." Mom raised a hand to stop them. "I can only fit so many in this room at one time. Leave the baskets outside in the carport."

They trudged back out and put the baskets up against the house, out of the golf cart's path. Then they filed back inside and plopped down on the stools at the kitchen bar.

"What do you need us to do, Mom?" Jan asked.

"It's a little too small of an area for four more people right now," Mom said. "And we've got a system going. Why don't you check outside with your father after you cool down?"

Before they could move, Dad walked in, followed by Caleb and the other men, and his voice drifted their way. "... does that make sense?"

"Yeah," Mr. Tilbrook replied. "Works by me."

The men moved into the kitchen. Dad kissed Mom while Mr. Tilbrook pulled the lid off the pot on the stove, then leaned in to take a whiff.

"Whoa, what is that?" He jerked his head back, his nose wrinkled and mouth screwed up. "Not supper, I hope."

The ladies laughed so hard tears streamed down their faces while he crossed his arms and scowled at them.

Mom dried her face and calmed enough to speak. "Pickle brine, sir. Dill pickles?"

When the ladies broke out laughing once more, the men joined in, chuckling at Mr. Tilbrook's expense.

His face reddened. "Oh."

"We've got a solid plan now." Mr. Boswell rescued Mr. Tilbrook. "Each team of two will take turns on watch."

Mr. Tilbrook nodded. "And we'll build a stand in the tree beside the house."

Caleb tugged at his hair. "Covering the watches and building the stand while still keeping up with the farm work is going to be a challenge."

Lizzy popped off her stool and into the conversation. "We can help with the farm work. We already got most of the cucumbers picked."

"Thata girl." Dad clapped her on the back. "We're going to put together a schedule, and everyone will do their part. It's going to take a team effort to make this work."

《》

On the first market day after Renee returned, Jan woke early, then nudged Renee in the makeshift bed beside her. "Out of bed, sleepyhead. Do you have any idea how much I've missed you at the auctions?"

Renee rolled onto her side, facing Jan, and tucked her hands under the pillow. "Been so long, I've almost forgotten how they smell!"

Like that could happen. Jan rolled her eyes and scrambled out of bed. "Dad's selling another set of steers today and hopes to pick up the building supplies for the watch stand. Maybe we'll find that others have moved back to the area like you have. You never know, there might be more of our classmates back. Wouldn't that be amazing? Let's hurry and get breakfast."

After breakfast, the men drove together in the truck while the rest of the group gathered in the golf cart for the ride. Jan sat beside Renee in the second-row seat. Lizzy talked a mile a minute in the third row while Jacob sat listening.

"Dad is going to talk to Officer Bradley today," Jan whispered to Renee. "To see what the police found out about Jacob's family."

"I feel so bad for him. I can't imagine being alone in the world." Renee glanced over her shoulder at the boy. "Does he ever talk about his family?"

Jan shook her head. "Never. Mom has tried so many times to ask him, and he clams up." Then she leaned closer to Renee's ear. "Officer Bradley said they'd look to see if there was any family left to claim him."

They'd arrived at the auction well after Dad and the other men had offloaded the steers at the barn, so they parked the golf cart behind the truck. Jan grabbed Renee by the arm and whispered, "Let's find Dad. Maybe we can find him before he talks to Officer Bradley."

They found Dad still in the auction barn. After he concluded his business with the manager, he wound his way through the maze of tables to Officer Bradley's car. Dad stepped up to the officer, who stood beside his vehicle, and shook his hand. "Afternoon, Officer. I wanted to check back with you to see what you'd found out about the boy."

The officer hooked his thumbs in his belt loops. "It's not what I was hoping for. It would be best if there was a clean break for the boy." He looked sideways at Jan and Renee as they stepped up beside Dad. "Unfortunately, the boy's mother is still alive. No one knows where she went, though."

"What do you mean, no one knows?" Jan broke in. "A mother doesn't just walk away from her kid."

Dad gave her a look to silence her.

Officer Bradley raised both hands as if saying, "Who knows?" "A friend on the Columbus police force did some investigating. He found the boy's old apartment and talked to the neighbors."

"Do they know how to find his family?" Jan dared to interrupt. If they could find even a single relative, then Jacob wouldn't be alone anymore.

"Unfortunately, no. It appears his grandparents are deceased. His father is an only child, and his mother had only one brother, the man we found dead in the truck."

Jan's stomach clenched at the thought of Jacob being so alone in the world. Seeming to sense her distress, Dad put his arm around her and pulled her in close to him.

"Mom left the boy with the uncle, and the neighbors hadn't seen her since. The uncle left with the boy about a month later. The neighbors said he couldn't pay the rent and got kicked out."

"So, we need to find his mom then," Dad said. "Any leads on her?"

"Only one. But it's not good." The officer lowered his voice and leaned in. "We think she joined that gang of marauders making their way from Columbus."

She gasped. Jacob's mother was a marauder!

Chapter Twenty

Dad squeezed her so tightly Jan couldn't breathe and squirmed to be set free.

"What will we do with the boy? We can't exactly go knocking on the door of a house the marauders have invaded," Dad said. "Just dropping off the boy!"

Officer Bradley stroked his stubbled chin. "It's a bit of a mess. We would have to sever the mother's rights before we could give him a permanent home." He bent his head and rubbed the back of his neck. "But how do we tell the boy? It's not easy to tell a young man his mom's a thief."

"Leave that to us." His arm still around Jan's shoulder, Dad patted her. "Marie knows how to connect with him. She'll figure it out."

The officer held up a hand. "There's something else, Steve. The gang is moving closer to your farm by the week. I expect you've already started preparing?"

Dad nodded. "We've got plans."

"Good. From what we're hearing from other police departments, they send a scout out first." He looked at her, frowned at her ponytail, then shook his head as if to clear the thought. "Word is that it's a redhead. A woman. If you see anyone like that on your place, you hold on to her. Get word to me. I'll collect her, and we'll use her to get this gang off the streets."

How in the world was Mom going to break this news to Jacob? He'd be devastated. Jan clamped her arms across her chest and took in slow breaths, not quite believing everything she'd heard. Once again, people were proving themselves untrustworthy.

What should have been a fun day was turning out to be a nightmare. Renee ribbed her and twitched her head to the side. Right.

"Dad, we're going to see what's out there for trade. Maybe we can trade some molasses for some of those pickles we brought," Jan said.

"Sure, just check back every hour with your mom. Make sure she doesn't need any help. Got it?"

"Yes, sir."

She was so grateful to have her best friend to escape with. She didn't want to think about marauders or mothers who abandoned their children anymore.

They were off. Arm-in-arm, they moved between the tables. There were rabbits to pet, boiled peanuts to sample, and tables to inspect. Halfway through the day, they stopped back at their table for one of their hourly check-ins. The pickles were half sold, and business appeared to be brisk.

"Need anything, Mom?" she asked.

"We're good, sweetie." Mom tucked wisps of dark hair behind her ears. "Did you find that molasses for trade?"

"Aw, sugarplum fairies! I forgot." She linked arms with Renee. They'd been having so much fun being together, they'd forgotten their only task for the day. "We'll go find it right now."

Mom crooked her finger at her, signaling for a close conversation. So Jan freed her arm and scooted over beside Mom, who whispered into her ear. "You need to take Lizzy with you. She shouldn't be stuck here while you girls are out having fun."

"Mo–om–mm." Jan dragged the word out so it had three syllables.

"Young lady?"

Now she'd done it. The "young lady" was out in the atmosphere. That was never a good sign.

"Yes, ma'am."

Mom snagged her shoulder and pulled her in closer to whisper. "You'd better make the invitation good, young lady. I don't want to be disappointed."

Yikes. Flashback to when she was six years old and in trouble for snubbing a cousin at a picnic. She'd spent the rest of the afternoon in time-out.

"Yes, ma'am."

She walked over to where Lizzy, chatting in her too-animated fashion, had just finished her latest transaction. "Hey, Lizzy. We're on the hunt for some molasses." When Renee joined them, Jan pointed between herself and her friend so there'd be no mistaking who the shoppers were. "We'd love for you to help us find it. After all, we've been out for half the day already with no luck."

Lizzy's eyes crinkled up as a smile stretched out her face so wide it must be painful. "Really? I'd love to. I'm sure I can help you find some. Did you know negotiation is one of my talents? Your mom even says so. You should ask her."

Just great. Negotiating was *Jan's* forte. Now would she have to step back and let diarrhea mouth bungle the bartering?

As they walked off, she turned back to see her mom's grin. When Mom waved and then snickered into her hand, Jan dared roll her eyes.

《》

The day was still early. Jan had just started her chores, and the chicken coop awaited her attention. Today's list included its thorough clean out with fresh bedding laid down afterward. Of all the chores, this was one of the easier ones.

To keep the shedlike building from getting too hot, they had placed it in the shade of a giant water oak. She started early to ensure she got as much done as possible before the heat grew unbearable. On the solo project, she had plenty of time to think while she shoveled smelly bedding out into a broken trough. The container would no longer efficiently hold water for the cattle, but it worked great to compost chicken manure mixed with bedding. She dumped red worms into the container at the beginning of each season to work the refuse, resulting in a beautifully composted soil supplement that grew strong, healthy vegetables every year.

Shovel down. Slide through the soiled litter. Lift the full scoop. Walk to the trough. Dump. Return for another load.

Mindless work. Lizzy talked a mile a minute all yesterday afternoon as they searched for the molasses. At first, the annoying rampage hammered in Jan's skull. The girl just didn't stop. But wouldn't you know it? Lizzy was the one who found the molasses. Not only that but she also negotiated a brilliant trade. She'd talked up the pickles so much Jan felt they were getting the raw end of the deal by trading four whole jars of pickles for only one jar of molasses. That girl really knew how to trade. She'd have made a great advertising agent. Jan snorted, not that she was looking for a teammate on that useless job.

Shovel down. Slide through the soiled litter. Lift the full scoop. Walk to the trough. Dump. Return for another load.

After they'd completed their syrup hunt, they'd spent the rest of the time exploring. Lizzy calmed enough to listen to Renee tell stories about living in Columbus. Once the girl stopped yammering, she was pleasant to have around. Who knew?

Shovel down. Slide through the soiled litter. Lift the full scoop. Walk to the trough. Dump. Return for another load.

Jan almost caught herself smiling. Life was feeling like it had before all the girls had left for the larger cities. Maybe someday it would be like it had been before. Was it possible life could return to the way it was before the variant? The average American never wanted for anything back then. People worked together. Students learned together. Sports teams competed against each other. Heaven.

Metal grated against wood as she scraped the last bits of soiled litter and shoveled it forward, out the door, and onto the ground. Two more scoops and she would have the entire pile in the trough.

Shovel down. Slide through the soiled litter. Lift the full scoop. Walk to the trough. Dump. Return for another load.

With the marauders headed toward them, they had to carry guns, set traps, and live in fear. She was tired of it.

She walked back to the toolshed beside the house, opened the door, and entered. The wheelbarrow leaned up against the inside wall. She hauled it down and crossed to the woodchip pile, then shoveled in clean litter.

Was it possible she needed to trust Jacob and Lizzy as much as she trusted Renee? Or would that end up being her second biggest mistake?

The wood chips spread easily in the coop, but the chickens kept coming in and out of the building, getting in her way. She closed the door and was dusting the chips off her jeans when a bang caused her to jump.

Oh no. The trip wire set off the first trap again. Now what?

She ran back to the house to ensure the men had heard the sound. Before she reached the porch, Dad sprinted out of the house, rifle in hand, Caleb on his heels. Mr. Boswell headed from the feeding pen, a handgun out at his side.

"Get in the house now," Dad ordered as he passed her.

With no need to respond, she was halfway to the door. The laundry room was open. Caleb must have ignored it on his way out. She dashed through it down the hallway to the kitchen. Mom was there with Mrs. Boswell. They had been cleaning up after breakfast, but Mom stood frozen in place, a kitchen towel hugged to her chest as if it were a baby needing protection.

"Where's Renee?" Jan asked. Renee's job was weeding this morning, along with Lizzy and Jacob. Had they gone out yet?

"We're here." Renee came down the stairway, Lizzy on her heels.

"Jacob?" Jan asked.

"Here." His head popped out of the bathroom, and he stepped out, belt hanging unbuckled as he zipped his pants.

That was everyone except for Mr. Tilbrook. She tried to visualize the chore calendar. What was his first task today?

Thoughts of calendars evaporated when shouting erupted outside. She ran back out through the front door and then down the porch steps. The yelling was coming from the driveway. Were they under attack?

Back into the house, she went. "Mom, get the gun and be ready. It doesn't sound good."

Mom's face paled further, but she dashed to the laundry room where the gun safe was still open from Dad and Caleb's withdrawals.

Another gunshot rang out. Then more shouting erupted

from the driveway, then silence. The silence was worse than anything else. What did it mean? They moved out to the porch and listened. Max and Luna howled in the distance—no, not in the distance. The noise was growing closer as the dogs were on their way to the action in the driveway.

Jan stood at the porch rail and pointed her handgun toward the driveway. Mom came up beside her and aimed the rifle in the same direction. Dad had taught them how to be ready, but her hands were shaking.

Please don't make me have to shoot someone. Please, God. I don't want to shoot anyone.

They waited. And waited.

Her wrist was killing her. The gun lowered ever so slightly, and with trembling hands, she jerked it back up, pointing it toward the driveway.

Then the tips of some heads came up over the rise. Her heart slammed in her throat. She might vomit.

The heads became faces—Dad, then Caleb, then a third person, struggling between the two of them. Mr. Boswell came up behind them, carrying his gun and watching left, right, and behind.

Thank you, God. They're okay. She lowered the gun, and Mom followed suit.

As they came closer, the third person became a woman with hair redder than Jan's spilling out of a filthy hat crammed on her head. Someone pushed past Jan—Jacob, wanting to get a peek.

He froze, staring at the person Dad and Caleb were wrestling to the house. He dropped the bat he'd been holding and stepped backward as if repulsed as he whispered something.

When he took another step backward, he backed into Jan, and

she put her hands on his shoulders. Then he spoke.

"Mom?"

Chapter Twenty-One

They all turned to Jacob. He stood statue-still, unable to take his focus off the woman.

The redhead jerked her head up at his voice. "Jacob!"

Her struggle for freedom intensified as if she were a wild animal caught in a trap.

"No!" Jacob yelled, then ran into the house.

"There are zip ties on top of the safe," Dad told Mr. Boswell. "Get two."

Mr. Boswell jogged inside.

"Let me go! I need to see my son." The woman tugged and jerked to escape their hold, turning Caleb's face bright red with the exertion of keeping her contained. On one lunge toward Dad, she bared her teeth, trying to reach his hands for a bite. Caleb yanked her back in time, but then she kicked at his shin. Dad jerked her back his way so the kick was futile.

Then Mr. Boswell emerged from the house, zip ties in his hands. "Got 'em."

"Let's put her down here, son," Dad said.

Caleb nodded as if responding to a plan they'd decided on earlier. They pinned her struggling arms behind her back, then pushed behind her knees to force her to the ground. Mr. Boswell shoved her shoulders down so she lay prone while Dad zip-tied her hands together.

Once they'd bound her, Dad leaned to her ear. "Look, you're already trussed up like a holiday turkey. We can do this the easy way or the hard way." When she stopped struggling, he continued. "The easy way means you behave and we help you stand back up, very ladylike."

She let out a squeal.

"The hard way means we bind your feet as well and carry you, like a pig on a spit. What's your pleasure?"

She screeched out another frustrated cry. A tear slid down her cheek as she stopped her struggles, then relaxed into submission.

"Okay, Caleb. Let's help the lady up."

They clambered off the ground. Then each grabbed her under the armpits and eased her up to a standing position.

"I want to see my boy." Once she was erect, her eyes pleaded with Dad. "Please."

He looked toward the house where Jacob had just run. "We'll see."

Jan followed as they marched the woman into the house, plopped her into one of the metal chairs, and zip-tied each ankle to a chair leg. Everyone crowded inside. Jacob was nowhere in sight.

"Please. My son. I need to see him." Tears created streaks of mud on the filth caking her skin. "I need to explain."

Dad stood, hands on hips. "We'll see. Caleb, go reset the trip wire like I taught you."

"Yes, sir." Caleb raced for the door.

"Remember to be cautious of the second trip wire!" Dad shouted to Caleb's retreating back, then nodded to Mr. Boswell.

"Watch her. She'll have a trick or two up her sleeve after her time with the marauders, so don't underestimate her."

"Got it." Mr. Boswell pulled out the wicker chair at the head of the table, faced it toward the woman, planted himself on the seat, and laid his rifle in his lap.

While they glared at each other as if squaring off, Dad rested a hand on Mom's arm. "I'm leaving to find Mr. Tilbrook. Keep everyone inside until I'm back." He picked up his rifle and headed out.

"Mom, I'm going to check on Jacob," Jan said. "Make sure he's okay."

The redhead lurched in her chair, twisting toward Jan. "Please, tell him I'm sorry. Tell him I need him to come here."

Without responding, Jan headed toward the bedroom Caleb shared with Jacob. Sobs were leaking through the door when she knocked. "Jacob? Can I come in?"

The sobs continued.

She knocked again.

"Jacob, I'm coming in."

When she eased the door open, Jacob was sitting on the edge of the bed. Eyes closed, tears streaming down his face, his sleeve covered in mucus from wiping his nose. He peered up at her, and his anguished face made her stomach flip.

She stepped over to the bed and sat beside him when he shuffled over to give her more room. Her arm went around his narrow shoulders as if it had a mind of its own. She squeezed him closer, which elicited another sob as he turned to her and accepted the comfort she offered.

"I guess I'm playing the role of Captain Obvious here… but that's your mom, huh?"

He huffed out a laugh.

"I figured as much." She gave him another squeeze. "Sorry, buddy. I can't imagine how you must feel."

He jerked away, mopping his eyes and then his nose with his sleeve. But a fresh round of tears flowed. "She didn't want me."

"How do you know? She wants to talk to you pretty bad." Jan tousled his red hair so much like her own. "What happened to you two, anyway? Why did she leave you?"

Again, he mopped his face with his sleeve. She pushed up and snagged a towel from the laundry basket in the corner. He accepted it and blew his nose with a loud effort. When he next spoke, he didn't sound as stuffed up.

"When Dad died, Mom had to go find work. She told me to stay with my uncle." He paused and used the towel once more to swipe at his eyes. "Uncle Mike didn't want to work. He said he worked hard enough all his life, and it was time someone owed him."

Jacob shrugged. "Mom used to say everyone needed to pitch in and she'd go find work and bring back money for more food. She told me to stay with Uncle Mike and be good until she got back."

He stopped talking, seeming lost in the memory.

Jan nudged him. "What happened next?"

"Nothing. She never came back. Uncle Mike said she didn't come back because she didn't want me. He said I had to work to make up because he got stuck having to feed me."

He choked up on the last words. She flinched at the raw emotions on display.

Then he lifted his chin. "So we went on the road, and Uncle Mike taught me how to steal."

"Did you ever hear your mom say she didn't want you? Or was it only your uncle who said that?"

He didn't answer right away. His fingers twisted the towel around his other hand, then off. Around, then off. Finally, his shoulders sloped. "If she wanted me, she would've come back. She never did. Uncle Mike said she found another boy and another family. She didn't want me anymore because I was bad. Because I was a thief."

Jan hugged him close as his tears and snot soaked through her T-shirt. Gross. But she didn't let go until he'd cried it out and wrenched away.

"Jacob." She caught his chin and eased it up to look eye to eye. "There are a lot of bad people in this world. Your uncle was one of them." When he closed his eyes to break the connection, she released his chin. "Just because your uncle was bad doesn't mean you are."

He wouldn't look at her.

"I've learned you can't trust everybody, just like you have. But you can trust me. Can I trust you?"

At that, he made eye contact. "You can. I won't steal anymore. I'm going to be the best farmer you ever saw and earn my food in the honest way. Promise."

She winked. "Let's go see what she says. Shall we?"

He mopped his face once more and scuffled after her from the bedroom, back down to the dining room.

As soon as the redheaded woman saw him, she squirmed to get away. "Jacob. Baby. Come over here. Let me tell you what happened."

When he looked up at Jan, a question squinching his eyes, she twitched her head toward the woman.

So he walked to the opposite side of the table and sat. He shut his lips tight as though waiting for an explanation. Jan moved to stand behind Mr. Boswell so, if anything should go wrong, she wouldn't be in the way.

The woman strained against her bonds, leaning toward him. "Baby, I'm so sorry I didn't come back. I know you were waiting for me."

No response from Jacob other than to frown at his hands in his lap.

"I was trying to get a job, baby. This woman said she had a job for me. Good work, she promised. But when I followed her, I found out it was a trap." A quiver surged over her, and she ducked her head, stringy locks of hair slinking over her cheeks as her voice dipped to a whisper. "They didn't let me go and made me do bad things. Terrible things."

Jacob appeared fixated on his lap. He said nothing.

"I tried to get away, over and over. When I broke free, I didn't stop running and hiding until I got back to our apartment. You and Uncle Mike were gone by then. I didn't know what to do or where to look when you weren't there. I'm sorry, baby."

The silence was painful for Jan to wait through. She bit back from asking so many questions. Why would the woman trust a man to watch her son, especially one who was too lazy to help support his sister and nephew? Why didn't she search, or at least call the authorities to search for Jacob?

But this was Jacob's time, not hers. If only he would ask even one tiny question. Perhaps they could have a conversation. Instead, he stood, looked at his mother, and then walked back to the stairs. His footsteps soon clomped up to the bedrooms.

The woman seemed to crumple into herself as her shoulders sagged into her chest and her head lowered toward her breastbone.

Mom walked into the room then. She must have been listening from the kitchen. Once she was beside the woman, she put her hand on her arm and whispered in her ear.

It felt like a betrayal. Why would her mother comfort this stranger who plotted to harm their family? At best, she'd have led marauders to their home to steal everything they had. At worst, none of them would have survived.

But Mom sat beside the woman, put her arm around her neck, and whispered prayers into her ear. Jan couldn't hear everything, but she knew Mom was praying for comfort and healing. Like this woman deserved any of that.

She went to find Jacob.

At the bedroom, the door was open, and the boy sitting on the bed, fiddling with a small vase she'd made in art class, years ago.

He looked up at her when she came in. "Caleb says you made this and those butterfly pictures in your room, says you took classes back in school. Can you teach me to draw?"

The abrupt change in topic threw her. As soon as she recovered, she smiled. "Of course I will." She'd used fabulous art programs to create those on the computer, but she had learned a few techniques in art class she could pass on to the boy. She plopped onto the bed beside him. "Don't you want to talk about your mom?"

He shook his head. She understood. It was too hard to talk about right now. Good thing an easier topic was at hand. "Want me to get some art pens and paper now?"

"Nah. You don't have to right now." A sad smile twisted his face. He placed the vase on the side table.

"Fair enough. But I'd like to." She nudged his shoulder with hers. "I need something pretty to think about too."

She headed toward her room. The closet held all the art supplies she'd been hoarding, afraid to use up, knowing she wouldn't be able to get any more for a long time. Before she could get to her room, she heard her father come in, yelling for everyone to come into the living room. She dashed back to get Jacob, and the two of them headed to the living room.

Mr. Tilbrook was with Dad, his face pale. Caleb was back from resetting the trip wires, so everyone was there except for Mr. Boswell, still on guard duty.

Once everyone assembled, Dad cleared his throat. "The marauders are next door, at the Boswells' house. It's time to kick our plan into high gear."

Chapter Twenty-Two

Officer Bradley arrived that evening to interrogate the prisoner. Dad had left a message for him, but with the phone service so sporadic, no one expected to hear the phone ring.

"Hold up at the top of the hill. I'll be up soon to release the trip wires," Dad said into the phone.

After a long afternoon, they freed Jacob's mother's right hand so she could eat. They also gave her the opportunity to use the washroom,with Mrs. Boswell and Mom in view. Although glad Jan hadn't had to watch someone else use the facilities, she understood the necessity.

Jacob stayed in his room the rest of the day and even ate his supper there. Normally, Mom wouldn't allow anyone to eat supper in their room unless they were sick. But she seemed to understand that he needed time alone, or at least away from his mother.

Now they waited for Dad and Officer Bradley so they could find out what would happen to their redheaded spy. They'd tied her feet to the chair again and her hands behind her.

Dad opened the front door and strolled in with his guest. As Officer Bradley removed his hat and nodded at them in the living room, Dad swept a hand toward their prisoner.

"Officer Bradley, meet Megan Dunwoody, Jacob's mother and the marauder scout we've been waiting for."

"It would be best if we took her out to my car for questioning." Officer Bradley twisted his hat in his hands. "We could use a little privacy."

Mr. Boswell stood, handed his gun to Dad, and cut the ties holding Mrs. Dunwoody's legs to the chair. When he cut the tie securing her hands behind her back, she sighed and rubbed her wrists.

"Unfortunately for you, that's only a small reprieve," the officer said. "You may now stand and turn around with your hands behind your back. I'll give you some new wrist bracelets for our walk to my car."

She did as instructed, and they headed out to his police car where he placed her in the back seat and left the door open as they spoke.

Man, what Jan would give to be a fly on the roof of that car. It would be nice to know if the story Mrs. Dunwoody gave the officer matched the one she'd given her son. Jan crossed the room and sank into a seat beside Renee, linking their arms together to build up her strength. As Renee scooted closer and rested her head on Jan's shoulder, Lizzy plunked down on Jan's other side, but miracle of miracles, the girl stayed silent. Perhaps all that talk spewed out so often because she'd been so long with no one to talk to. Jan slid her hand over and clasped Lizzy's, gathering strength from her presence as well.

After what seemed like an eternity, the police officer closed the patrol car's rear door and returned to the house. They were all waiting for him in the living room. Jan opened the door for him. No need to knock when they were all eager to hear what he could get out of the prisoner.

"As they always say—I've got good news, and I've got bad news." He removed his hat and dropped it on the oak coffee table, then claimed one of the metal dining room chairs someone had brought in. "The good news is she appears to be cooperating. Says she'll do anything to keep her son safe now that she knows where he is."

Jacob wandered into the room, and Officer Bradley looked right at him now.

"The bad news is the marauders will wonder where she's gone. Most likely, they'll search each of the homes she was to scout when she doesn't return to them tonight. So you folks don't have long to make up a plan."

Dad rubbed his stubbled chin, his dry palm creating a scratch-ing sound as it scraped against the bristles. "We've got a plan figured out, but having an extra man on hand to carry it off would be great."

"You might need more than one more person to handle this gang." The officer drummed his fingers on his thighs. "They've got twice your number and are armed pretty well, from what she says."

Dad surveyed his crew, then leveled his focus on Bradley. "We've got home-court advantage, as they say. And our plan is solid. But we're happy to have more people on our side if you know of any."

Officer Bradley peered out at his car. "I've got a dozen other officers in the surrounding area. I'm not sure how many can make it here before the gang comes, but I'll call around. We'll see."

They brought Jacob's mom back into the house, and the officer shared watch duty.

«»

Five other police officers responded to the backup request, so breakfast was a huge affair. Now they all gathered around the kitchen and dining room area talking strategy.

The chatter of the women scrambling eggs and the aroma of frying bacon emanated from the kitchen. It took dozens of eggs to feed everyone. Without enough space, they'd eaten in turns at the dining room table.

The fresh faces roaming around enthralled Jan. She hadn't seen this many people in a private residence since a family reunion when she was small. Energized by so much going on, she could pretend they were at a pep rally. Conversations varied from room to room, and she let herself jump from one group to the next to experience them all.

With their plan ready and trip wires reset, the men patrolled the fence lines by foot and golf cart, and the dogs ran the fence once an hour. So far, no one had spotted any intruders.

Officers continued to interrogate Mrs. Dunwoody. Though she asked to speak to Jacob, he never agreed to sit with her and remained out of eyesight. Jan worried about him. Thinking you were alone in the world, then having your mother reappear couldn't be easy. He still didn't want to be near her. Jan shivered, thinking how much it would have hurt her to reject her own mom.

One officer called the others together, and they spoke in hushed tones. Once again, Jan went all twitchy, wishing she could hear what was being said. Not that they'd talk in front of a "little lady." She rolled her eyes at Lizzy, wondering if the chatterbox felt the same way.

After the group conferred, Officer Bradley ambled over to Dad and murmured something. The rest of the men gathered in the group, including Caleb. Jan snuck over to listen, but Dad made eye contact and shook his head.

"Go see what your mother and the ladies in the kitchen need, kiddo."

Shoot. Why did Caleb get to listen in, but she didn't? Not fair.

She stomped into the kitchen like a petulant child. *If they want to treat me like a baby, then I can act like one.* The ladies were cleaning up and murmuring.

"It's got to be difficult to think of those hooligans in your home, Helen." Mom placed a hand on Mrs. Boswell's forearm. "Just the thought of them going through my home, my personal space, gives me the creeps."

"If I could march over there and chase them all out with a broom, I'd do it in a heartbeat." Mrs. Boswell flicked long blond bangs out of her eyes and scraped lard from a frying pan. "I'm just glad we brought all the food over here, along with everything that was really important to us."

Renee snitched a broken bit of muffin from the countertop. "You'd think they'd move on since there isn't any food." She popped the crumb in her mouth. "Isn't that what they're after?"

Lizzy plunged a stack of plates into the soapy sink. "They're probably after most anything they can find. Hopefully, they don't trash the place or burn it down like they did that farm in Waverly Hall."

Renee blanched.

Dad strode into the kitchen. "Where's Jacob?"

"In his room, as usual." Jan froze. "Why?"

"His mom agreed to help us out for leniency on her part in the crime spree," Mr. Boswell said as he entered the room. "She wants to speak to the boy one more time before she heads back to the gang."

"That's not fair." Jan bristled, taking a step closer to Dad and crossing her arms over her chest. "He didn't agree to speak to her."

"We won't force him, kiddo." Dad rested his hands on her upper arms, his voice soothing. "We're just going to ask him if he wants to talk. That's it. It's his choice."

Asking him that right now didn't seem fair. He'd holed up in his room since their first conversation. Couldn't they see he wanted nothing to do with her? "Let me talk to him." Jan's shoulders sloped as her arms swung loose. "If he wants to come out, I'll let you know."

"Okay." Dad patted her. "But don't put negative thoughts into his head. Let him decide on his own."

Fair enough. She went to knock on Jacob's door.

The door wasn't closed, and he sat on the bed looking through notes she'd made from her Studio in Art course.

"Hey, Jacob." She moved into the room and sat at the foot of the bed.

"Hey." He eyed her warily, closed the binder and placed it on the bedside table, then moved to sit beside her.

"Your mom has agreed to help the police capture the gang."

He leaned into her but said nothing.

"There's one catch." She elbowed his arm. "She's asked to speak to you again."

His head jerked up, eyes wide.

"You don't have to. I told Dad you probably didn't want to talk to her." As he visibly relaxed, she stifled the urge to put an arm around him. "But you never know what might happen to her when she returns to the gang. You may never get another chance to ask her questions. So think about it before you say no. Okay?"

Before Jacob could respond, Mom popped her head through the doorway. "Can I have a minute, Jacob?"

At his nod, she sat on his other side and placed the pillow she held into his hands. "I made this for myself a few years ago. I'd like you to have it now."

Jacob ran an index finger over the embroidered words.

Jan leaned down to catch his eye. "It's from the Bible—'Love prospers when a fault is forgiven, but dwelling on it separates close friends, Proverbs 17:9.'"

He raised questioning eyes to Mom.

"When I made that pillow, I was struggling to forgive a friend for something she did to hurt me. I thought I'd never be able to get over it." Mom patted his knee, then brushed her hand over the raised letters on the pillow. "Each day, as I worked on the pillow, I prayed to understand why I should forgive the person who'd hurt me. By the time I finished, I had my answer. Forgiveness isn't for the other person. It's for the person who has the forgiving to do."

He scrunched his nose like he'd tasted something sour, then spit out the question: "But why?"

"Because when we forgive others, it frees our hearts to love again. And love heals." She slipped her arm around him and pulled him into a hug. "You don't have to trust your mom again, Jacob, but if you forgive, it will heal you and make you feel so much better in here." She touched his chest over his heart.

He put his small hand over hers. "If I talk to her, will you both stay with me when I do?"

"Of course," Jan said. Mom signaled agreement.

He let out a heavy breath as if taking on an immense weight. Then, gripping the pillow against his chest, he rose from the bed and headed for the door, Jan and Mom close behind.

When the men saw him coming, they moved out of his way so he could reach his mother unimpeded. As he took the seat opposite her at the table once again, Jan and Mom flanked him.

No longer tied to the chair, Mrs. Dunwoody smiled at her son. The smile never lightened her sad eyes. "I know how disappointed you must be in me, Jacob." She swiped a tear from her eyes. "You should know I'm probably more disappointed in myself than you are in me."

Jacob squeezed the pillow even tighter to his chest.

"If you never forgive me, I understand." She let out a tiny laugh. "But no matter what, I want you to remember I am sorry I made wrong choices. Someday, I hope you'll have a son of your own. Then maybe you'll understand how parents aren't perfect."

He slid closer to Jan in his chair.

"If that day ever comes, please remember that I love you. I never stopped loving you. And I never will stop loving you until the day I die."

Officer Bradley tapped Mrs. Dunwoody's shoulder. "It's time to go now."

She stood and smiled once more at Jacob. "Goodbye, baby. I hope to see you again, real soon."

They escorted her out the door.

Chapter Twenty-Three

Jan's heart skipped a beat as a single tear slid down Jacob's cheek when they escorted Mrs. Dunwoody out. When he lowered his head and wiped the tear on the pillow, she nudged him with her shoulder. "Are you okay?"

He nodded. "What are they doing with my mom?"

More pooled tears threatened to overflow from his red eyes.

"She's going to help us, remember?" Jan pushed up from her seat. "I'll go see if I can find out more details."

She walked onto the front porch where the men clustered around their prisoner. She moved to stand beside her father, who wrapped an arm around her shoulders.

Officer Bradley shared a hand-drawn map of the property. "The tree beside the house is the best location to spot anyone approaching from a different angle than the driveway."

He pointed to a crude stick-figure tree in the diagram.

I could draw a better tree in my sleep.

Then he traced a line back to the driveway on the map, where someone had drawn two thin lines a few inches apart.

"If they set off both traps in the driveway, they'll most likely fan out around the driveway instead of taking the direct route." He tapped the map. "From what Megan says, they aren't the sharpest tools in the shed, but they learn from their mistakes."

He then pointed to one man. "I need you to take point to watch the trip-wire area. If you see them coming past the warning sign, hoof it back here behind the traps. Give the signal to our tree-stand watcher."

He raised one finger and twirled it in a circle above his head to demonstrate before facing Mr. Tilbrook. "You'll take the tree stand. When you see that signal, alert Caleb, who will patrol the house. Caleb, then ring that dinner bell one time—once, hear me?"

Officer Bradley straightened his shoulders, standing tall enough to block the morning sunbeams slanting through the east-facing porch. "The rest of us will be strategically located at the various perimeter gates. If that bell rings, move clockwise one station. Walk the fence line from your first assigned post to the next."

He slid his finger along the map in a circular motion, tapping at each of the gates on the outside fencing. "If you see anyone, keep out of sight. Watch and follow. If anyone sees you, then bring them in, using force if necessary. Of course, if there are multiple people and you need to alert the team to a breach, shoot your gun in the air so we'll know where they are coming from."

Then he lowered the map and rested his large hand on Mrs. Dunwoody's shoulder. "Megan, you know what to do?"

She bobbed her head. "I'm going up the driveway and around the corner to the Boswell property. Once I'm back inside, I'll tell them about this house and the farm, then lead them to the driveway and tell them it's clear sailing to the house." She shrugged at Dad. "They won't be able to resist the thought of fresh beef for dinner. Sorry, Steve."

Dad let out a brief harrumph.

"Remember." Officer Bradley eyed Mrs. Dunwoody. "Sell them the idea that the family here is nice and friendly. They fed you a sumptuous meal and let you stay overnight. No threats here, right?"

"Got it," she said.

Jan clenched her fists. It sounded a lot like what her son must've told his uncle.

"Everyone to their posts, then." Officer Bradley rubbed his hands together. "Let's do this."

Dad escorted Mrs. Dunwoody up the driveway, likely making sure she made it past the trip wires. The other men scattered along various paths to their stations.

Max and Luna sat beside Caleb. He bent down and rubbed each under their muzzles. Then he spoke firmly, "Okay, guys, it's time." He stood and pointed toward the fence line. "Hunt."

They tore off toward the fence line as if the best game ever had just begun.

She left him to his duty and went back inside. Jacob was still at the table, waiting with Mom.

"Your mom is being really brave." Jan sat down in the chair Mrs. Dunwoody vacated not long before. "She's going to tell the marauders it's safe to come here and lure them into our trap."

Jacob sprang out of his chair. "But if she brings them here, we won't be safe. What if she tells them about the traps? You can't trust her."

Mom grasped his arm as if needing to keep him from running away. "No. Your mother wouldn't do anything to put you in more danger, Jacob. I could tell she was sorry about leaving you."

Jan rubbed a chill from her arms, wishing she could chase

Mrs. Dunwoody down and give her more time to break through to the boy's aching heart. "I'm going to check on Caleb and make sure he doesn't need anything."

It felt like being torn in two. She wanted to stay with Jacob and comfort him, but she also needed to help defend her home and those she loved. Leaving her brother alone outside hurt worse than abandoning Jacob right now. Mom could care for the needs inside better than Jan could anyway.

She stepped back outside, shutting the door on the pain Jacob was feeling.

Caleb paced the length of the wraparound porch. "I'm on watch. Why don't you wait inside where it's safer?"

"I want to help too. I can stay here with you." She put her hands on her hips and then patted the gun she wore every day. "Better two sets of eyes than one."

He sighed as if dealing with a petulant child, which made her more determined to help. When she glared and stood her ground, his face relaxed. "Say, I know how you can help. Go up to the second floor and stake out the window facing the driveway. You'll have a better vantage point up there to let me know as soon as you see something coming."

That was actually a good idea.

"I can move from window to window instead of just watching one," she said. "In fact, I'll put everyone inside the house on window-watching duty so we'll be observing all sides."

"Even better." Caleb winked.

She dashed inside and informed the nervous occupants of the plan. Then each person claimed a window and dispersed. Mom stayed behind and went to the laundry room, crooking her finger at Jan. There, she opened the safe and pulled out the rifle she'd been practicing with and a box of bullets.

"I'm afraid this day won't end without someone getting hurt. You and I need to be on prayer guard as much as we are on watch for marauders. Shall we begin now?"

Jan bowed her head, knowing Mom would begin the prayer.

"Father, we don't want anyone to get hurt today, but we also don't want our farm to be taken from us." Mom draped her arm on Jan's shoulder, and the corner of the bullet box poked her. "You've blessed us with this farm and given us the knowledge and ability to work the land. We have friends in our lives to share with and to help us harvest the bounty. For that, we thank you and praise you."

Jan shifted her weight to the opposite foot as Mom's arm pressed down.

"Please protect everyone and help the men take the gang into custody with no one being injured or killed. Amen."

"Amen," Jan responded.

Tears pooled in Mom's eyes. Instead of indulging in them, she straightened her spine and rubbed Jan's back. "Okay, then. Let's do this." She headed for her own window.

It was hard not to think of the danger, but if Jan allowed herself the luxury of tears, she wouldn't have the fortitude she needed right now.

Her chosen window—the game room—overlooked the chicken coop and the driveway. With the trees surrounding the property, she couldn't see far, but she could discern a few of the men at their stations, Mr. Tilbrook in his tree stand, and Caleb below as he circled the house on his patrol.

The chickens pecked at the ground around their coop for bugs in the grass. If they understood the danger, they'd be hiding in the coop or under the front porch. If the gang made it through and took over the farm, the chickens would all end up in stewpots.

«»

All twitchy again, Jan jigged in place. It felt like she'd been standing at the window for hours. Her legs were restless just standing there with her staring out the window. Caleb had to have paced past her window fifty times, and his stride was slow.

Mr. Tilbrook looked uncomfortable in the tree stand, shifting from leg to leg. Occasionally, they'd smile at each other. Maybe the gang wouldn't be coming here today after all.

Then movement caught her eye. Mr. Tilbrook had gone still in his tree and stared at the driveway. The officer assigned to the driveway jogged toward the house, one finger up on the hand he circled in the air to catch Mr. Tilbrook's attention. Mr. Tilbrook waved back.

At that, the officer headed back toward the trip wires.

Mr. Tilbrook made a hoot-owl call.

I had no idea Mr. Tilbrook could do a hoot owl. He's pretty good at it.

Caleb jogged around the corner of the house, and Mr. Tilbrook circled one finger above his head, alerting him. Caleb acknowledged by circling his finger in the air, then sprinted toward the front of the house.

After one more quick look at the driveway, seeing nothing, Jan went to alert the others, heading first to her own room in the back of the house, where her mother stood at her assigned post.

"They're coming." She wasn't sure why she whispered it since there was no way someone coming down the driveway could hear her. But it felt right—stealthy.

"Driveway?" Mom gripped both arms of the desk chair she sat in and pushed herself up as she spoke in a responding whisper.

"Yup."

Mom strode to the doorway. "I'll move to your spot. Let everyone else know to keep an eye out. We need to be sure they aren't coming from other areas as well."

The dinner bell rang one time. The alarm.

"Will do," Jan said.

Mom bustled out of the room, taking her rifle and the box of bullets. Jan went from room to room on the second floor, alerting everyone. The gang, or at least a part of it, headed toward them via the driveway. They needed to keep a keen eye out for any others who might circle via other routes.

After she had put everyone on notice, Jan headed back to her mom. The gun shell went off in the first trap. At least she had to assume it was the trap. Why else would there be a single gunshot?

Please, God, let it be just the trap and not someone getting shot.

Change of plans. She headed downstairs. Caleb was alone on the porch, and she was going to back him up.

At the front door, she checked out the window. Caleb wasn't in sight, so she eased open the door and craned around for him—nowhere.

Since he wasn't on the porch, he must be on patrol around back. She'd watch the front until he could make his circle. She scanned the driveway and stiffened as an officer skulked through the trees. He appeared to be stalking the driveway as he progressed toward the house.

Oh no.

He started moving her way. Did that mean the gang was continuing down the driveway, ignoring the signs and the shotgun warning?

"Please, God, I don't want anyone to get hurt today. Turn them back around somehow."

The officer paused in his retreat and gave another signal to Mr. Tilbrook in the tree. Two fingers this time, with a chopping motion.

From the tree stand came another owl hoot. Unsure what this second alarm meant, she pivoted toward Caleb's footfalls as he ran around the side of the house. He sprinted onto the porch and struck the dinner bell three times.

Then came a sudden eruption of neighing horses and shouts and screams from the driveway.

She recalled what Caleb's signal meant. They'd tripped the second wire.

Chapter Twenty-Four

No way could they have set off the second trip wire without getting hurt—badly. And with the screams now emanating from the driveway, they'd suffered significant injuries.

Nauseated, Jan drew in a slow breath to hold her stomach down. Why did they have to be such idiots and ignore the warnings?

She slid her gun from her holster and readied herself for whatever came next. Men were running from their various perimeter posts. Max's and Luna's howls drew closer as the dogs heard the horses and screams and headed toward the action.

"What do I do next?" she asked Caleb.

He glowered at her. "You're supposed to be on window watch. Get there."

Right. Like that was going to happen.

She stood firm. It would take a lot more than his growling at her to move her from his side.

Then two people headed down the driveway. One walked behind the other, and the one in front had red hair. Mrs. Dunwoody!

As they neared, the person behind her became clearer. He

held a gun to her head with her shirt collar wrapped in his fist. An officer from the woods was creeping up behind them, his gun targeting the man's head. The duo reached the chicken coop, and the man shouted to Caleb.

"You must have met my friend, Megan, here."

The man yanked up on Mrs. Dunwoody's shirt collar. As she brought her hands up and struggled to free herself, her face grew redder by the second.

"I say," the man shouted, "because Megan seems to have known there was a second trap. She avoided being in front when it went off. Lucky for me, I saw the little minx move back and followed her just in the nick of time." He yanked the shirt collar even tighter, and Mrs. Dunwoody rose on her toes now, trying to relieve the choke hold. "Lucky me, huh?"

Dad ran up behind Caleb, and both now had their guns out and pointed toward the pair. More men arrived at the scene one at a time. Each targeted the couple in their sights.

Jan's heart was pounding, and her palms sweating against the gun grips. *Oh, please, God. Let this end.*

Officer Bradley arrived, gun out and trained on the man. All froze in their stance, waiting. "Sir, we can end this peacefully, but not if you kill someone." He took a step toward them. "Let Megan go, and we'll talk about getting you some food. You look hungry."

The man jerked at Mrs. Dunwoody's shirt again. Her lips were turning blue, and her eyeballs were rolling up into her skull. She was going to pass out.

Someone dashed out of the house, past Jan. When he was halfway to the couple, Jan gasped. It was Jacob.

"No! Let my mom go." He didn't pause in his headlong run toward the couple.

His mother's eyes went wild as her captor released her shirt to aim at Jacob.

"Little brat!" The gunman squeezed the trigger.

As the gun went off, Mrs. Dunwoody raised her elbow to hit the man's arm. Weapons fired all around the field. With such sound reverberating, surely everyone who had a gun shot at someone.

Stunned by the deafening noise and quick-turning events, Jan screamed.

The shooter and Mrs. Dunwoody fell to the ground, as did Jacob.

"Jacob!" Jan ran toward the boy, her heart slamming into her throat. No, not Jacob. He was just a kid. *Please, God, not Jacob.*

Dad grabbed her arm as she tried to run by him. "No."

She twisted her arm, trying to get away. "Jacob!"

"It's not safe. Wait."

The men all closed in around the pair on the ground. Dad strode toward the boy, gun extended as he appeared to be watching for any movement from the fallen gang member.

Did it have to take *forever* for Dad to reach Jacob's side? The boy was already getting up, his nose bloody, a welt growing on his jawline. Tears flowed down his face.

"Did you get shot? Where does it hurt, son?" Dad helped him to his feet.

"Mom"—the whimper warbled across the yard—"Mom, no."

When Jacob tried to get to his mother, Jan grabbed him by the sleeve. She inspected the boy and found no damage besides his face. She then saw the tree root that must have tripped him and a bloody stone where his face made contact when he fell.

CHAPTER TWENTY-FOUR

No bullet holes.

Thank you, God.

Officer Bradley had reached the couple and kicked away the man's gun. He signaled to the rest of the group that it was safe. Half of the officers moved up the driveway, guns drawn, to inspect the scene of the second trap. The other half came in and held guns on the gang member while an officer cuffed the man's limp form. Officer Bradley turned his attention to Mrs. Dunwoody.

As Dad started toward the downed couple, Jan followed while holding Jacob's hand. Mrs. Dunwoody's head turned to the side, and Jacob broke free of Jan's grasp.

"Mom!"

By the time Jan arrived at his side, blood from a bullet wound in his mother's shoulder covered Jacob too. Mrs. Dunwoody was sitting up, crushing her son in an embrace despite her wound.

Jacob wept in his mother's arms. "Mom, I forgive you. I'm sorry."

She rubbed his back with her hand, soothing him. "I'm so sorry, baby. I'm so sorry. I'll never leave you again."

Jan fell to her knees, a single refrain drumming through her pulse. *Thank you. Thank you.*

Mrs. Dunwoody was alive, Jacob had his mother again, and the men had stopped the marauders.

«»

That evening, they all sat in the house, discussing the day over a simple meal of cowboy cornbread, compliments of Caleb.

When Jan went to her bedroom, the door was ajar, and she peeked in. Mrs. Dunwoody, bandaged, lay on one side of the bed, and Jacob curled up to her with her arm around him on the other side. They were both sound asleep.

Jan closed the door behind her. Seeing the two of them together was such a relief. Returning to the dining room, she got a plate and scooped out a serving of the casserole. She took a seat within listening distance of the dining table where Officer Bradley was speaking.

"Thankfully, we had an accurate collection of shots fired." He surveyed the group. "Doc said the guy took ten bullets to center mass while Megan only took one to the shoulder. That guy never had a chance and most likely died instantly from wounds. She's lucky to be alive with so many guns pointed at them. You rarely get such accuracy in a gunfight like that."

One more thing to be thankful for.

"Will she be going to jail after she recovers?" Dad asked.

"She's proven she learned her lesson." Officer Bradley waved a dismissive hand. "Most of the gang is out of commission thanks to your second trap."

Dad acknowledged his role with a nod.

Then Officer Bradley leaned back in his chair, stretching his legs out and crossing them at the ankles with an air of contented accomplishment. "We arrested two who couldn't escape because of their injuries. From their interrogations, we know a few got away. But it's unlikely they'll come back to this farm. They might leave the area entirely. Even if they don't, there aren't many left."

A hand clasped Jan's wrist. Mom nodded toward the master bedroom, then headed toward it. Jan followed.

Once they were both in the room, Mom picked up the finished pillow she'd been embroidering all month. When she sat on the bed and patted the mattress beside her, Jan joined her and snuggled close, accepting the arm that enfolded her in a warm hug.

"I've been working on this for you, sweetie." Mom handed the pillow over, and Jan ran her hand across the embroidered words—*I am sending you out like sheep among wolves. Therefore, be as shrewd as snakes and as innocent as doves (Matthew 10:16).*

"Thanks, Mom. It's beautiful." A tear escaped and rolled down her cheek, but Jan smiled.

"You've been struggling to deal with trust ever since Jacob stole the truck." Mom smoothed the pillow on Jan's lap. "This is a reminder you don't have to push everyone away to be safe. You just have to be careful."

"I know, Mom. I get it."

"Before Jacob came into our lives, you used to love auction and market day." Mom jostled their shoulders together. "It wasn't supplies you needed to sustain you, but friends. You were always on the hunt for another to join your group. 'The more the merrier,' you always said."

The memory of the times she and Renee had contests on market day warmed Jan. Who could fist bump the most people at the tables? Jan always won, but her friend gave her a run for the money.

Mom grasped Jan's shoulders and turned Jan to face her. "You've learned your lesson about trusting everyone blindly. But perhaps you've taken the lesson too much to heart." Mom pressed on Jan's chest, over her heart. "It's time to let it go now. Time to let others besides Renee back in. You've got Lizzy and Jacob. They both need you. What do you say?"

Jan closed her eyes. What if Jacob had been too late to forgive his mother? What if she'd died? He'd never have had another chance. Jan couldn't imagine such weight on her soul.

Mom was right—as usual. It was time to let go of the hurt

and the anger and bring others into her new posse of friends.

"You're right. I've been an idiot." Standing up, she moved to the door. "I need to make amends with Lizzy."

"I like the sound of that, sweetie."

Jan hugged the pillow to her chest as she wandered back to the group. With so many eating, they filled the kitchen, dining room, and living room. Lizzy and Renee were in the kitchen, laughing at a joke Caleb told.

"What a ham." Jan punched her brother in the arm. "You always have at least one joke up your sleeve."

She then moved to stand beside Lizzy, who sat on a stool in front of a half-eaten bowl of cowboy cornbread, smiling at Caleb's joke.

Lizzy smiled at her, and Jan winked back. Having friends again was going to be fun.

Chapter Twenty-Five

People filled the auction and market grounds, haggling for the best deal on goods being offered. It had been a long time since such a crowd gathered at the auction lawn. Mom, Mrs. Boswell, and Mrs. Dunwoody all worked at the table, selling pickles, Caleb's whittling projects, and freshly canned green beans.

Jan walked beside Renee while on Renee's other side Lizzy chatted in her rapid-fire way. Jan could barely keep up with the conversation. On her opposite side, Jacob held a bunny they'd traded for. Jan held a second rabbit, soft and cuddly. Holding the animal without stroking its silken fur was impossible.

The house had gotten even more crowded. Mrs. Dunwoody had recovered enough to help with chores. Jacob had transformed into a regular chatterbox, taking on the role of Jan's little brother. Caleb, off looking for the cute blonde, wouldn't allow a tail. Otherwise, Jacob would be at his idol's side. Funny how the young boy looked up to her brother so soon after joining the family again.

"Are you sure we got both a girl bunny and a boy bunny?" Jacob looped ahead, then pivoted to walk backward in front of her. "Caleb said we had to have one of each if we wanted babies."

She giggled. "Yes, I looked."

"I can't wait for babies. We'll have fuzzies all around us. I call dibs on the first one." If he didn't turn around soon, he'd walk into someone.

She didn't have the heart to tell him most likely the babies would end up being stew. They didn't have time or space on the farm for pets. She'd let Dad explain it when the time came.

Lizzy skipped in front of her. "Want to get some taffy? Dad gave me some money. It's not much, but probably enough for a piece for each of us."

Ever since she'd let Lizzy into her heart, their friendship had grown. Lizzy was like another sister—an annoying one at times, but also appreciated for her enthusiasm for life. Jan's family had expanded to include everyone who lived with them.

The men had talked of the Boswells moving back home, and the Tilbrooks were going to move their RV back to the old spot on the Boswells' property. As soon as they could get another set of dogs to patrol the expanded area, they'd make the move. Though they'd all still work the farm together, it would be a lot quieter when everyone moved out.

"I'd love a piece of taffy," Jacob piped up.

And Jan's heart soared on a rush better than a sugar-high or pep rally. Once again, she was a part of an enormous family of friends. Having her own posse and knowing she wouldn't be alone anymore felt right. What a blessing. Who said the world didn't have as much as it used to? On days like this, it felt like she had more than ever.

The End

Take a sneak peek
   at the next installment!
   Honor

Collapse Book 2: Honor ~ Prologue

Caleb Worthington opened his eyes to nothing but blackness. He blinked twice, thinking he must not be fully awake. Still black. His head pounded with the worst headache ever. When he tried to raise his hand to massage the ache, he couldn't. Someone had bound them together.

His heart raced as his throat dried and choked him. He tried to rise, but they'd tied his feet as well. What was going on here? Where was he?

Stop. Think. What's the last thing you remember?

He'd been at market day. Mom was minding the table with their neighbor, Mrs. Boswell. Jan, Renee, and Lizzy had taken Jacob on a hunt for a lamb. Dad, Mr. Boswell, and Mr. Tilbrook were at the auction to see what price their heifers would bring in.

At least Caleb could remember these specific details, even though he couldn't remember where he was or how he'd gotten here. He wasn't a full-on amnesiac. He knew he just turned nineteen. And he had a girlfriend. Sort of.

Man, it was dark in here—and hot. Had someone stuck him into a huge oven? Like the fairy-tale witch who planned to bake Hansel and Gretel.

Okay. Now you're losing it, dude. It is highly unlikely you are in a fairy tale.

Dad would tell him to think his way out of the problem and

not go all "bull in a china shop." Time to rethink the situation. Slow deep breaths, in and out. What *did* he know about his surroundings?

He was lying down somewhere hot, bound hand and foot. The floor felt like wood, and he'd swear there was a splinter in the back of his hand. No noises offered to help him with location. Not even a breeze or other air movement, so he had to be inside something. A cabin, perhaps? Whatever it was, it had no air conditioning, but few places had electricity these days.

He squirmed and tried to sit up. Success!

Now to figure out where he was. He inchwormed a foot or so until he reached a wall. It scratched like plywood against his cheek. Perhaps a shed? But how did he land in a shed, tied-up, with a massive headache? He pushed his head against the wall to steady himself and turned to use the wall to lean against. Shoot! As the back of his head contacted the wall, a raised welt throbbed. That explained the headache.

Perhaps someone was nearby, waiting for him to wake. Should he announce he was awake by calling out? Probably not a good idea. After all, if he was tied up and someone was waiting for him, it wasn't for a surprise party. Especially with the love tap on his head.

Dad would say he should pretend to be asleep and see if he could surprise whoever showed up.

Mom would tell him to pray. She had such a deep faith. Whenever something bad was going down—whether illness, injury, or wayward actions—she jumped right in with prayer. Even when Dad needed supplication, Mom prayed for him and ignored his unbelief.

Man, it was hot in here. Wherever here was.

Caleb wasn't sure what to believe since Dad was silent in

his protest against God, the exact opposite of Mom's vocal devotion. He sure wanted to believe right now, though.

If God existed, he wasn't happy with Caleb. He'd sure messed things up.

Conversely, prayer couldn't hurt anything. Especially if it was a whispered one.

"God, if you are out there listening, I could use a hand here. Not sure how I got into this wooden furnace, all trussed up like a Thanksgiving turkey. I'd sure appreciate a way out. If it's okay with you, I'm going to hold off on ending this prayer, so I'll save the amen for later, when this is over."

He put his ear to the wall and listened. Nothing. Next, he lay back down and rolled to his side to listen on the floor. Still nothing.

Shoot. This wasn't helping. He needed to think. What was the last thing he remembered doing at the auction?

Thinking hurt, but he powered through the pain. *Engage your brain, Caleb!*

He'd helped unload the heifers Dad planned to sell today. At least he assumed it was still the same day. Hard to tell in this pitch-black room.

After they'd unloaded, they'd gotten the receipt from the attendant. Since the auction was going to start soon, he'd gone to grab a seat at the highest bench overlooking the auction pit. When he'd sat down, someone joined him. Someone he was happy to see. Who?

Sweat was rolling down his brow, and his mouth was cottony dry. It was so hot. Had someone put him in here to bake him to death? Why else would they leave him in this heat with no access to water? Why tie him up and lock him in a room? It made little sense.

Who had he met up with? That had to be important.

Head hurts. Thirsty. Hot.

Emma! Figures. The word *hot* would remind him of her. With her curly blond hair and bright blue eyes, she was stunning. He could spend all day thinking about her, holding her hand, or gazing into her eyes. *Hello! Earth to Caleb. Get back to the problem, man.*

Emma had sat with him. She'd run up the stairs to say hello and then joined him through the bidding. There weren't many heads to sell today, if it was still today, so the sale had ended quickly. They'd gotten a decent price for the heifers too, since there weren't many to buy. Dad would be happy about that. Would be happy or was happy? The sale was over a long time ago, maybe. Was Dad looking for him now?

A cramp seized his left leg, a result of his unforgiving position, and his wrists burned. They must've used zip ties on him. The plastic dug into his skin. Soaked with sweat, he couldn't tell if the fluid on his hands was perspiration or if blood oozed from the wounds scraped into his skin.

What happened after Emma joined him? He was happy with the sale, and she'd smiled and winked one of those beautiful blues. He'd never forget that wink. As if they shared in a secret. Maybe it was time to ask her out on an official date.

Though, come to think of it, she hadn't told him where she lived. Hopefully, it was within range of their electric golf cart. No way Dad would lend him the truck for a date.

Okay, hotshot. Stop thinking about the girl. You are in a pickle here. Focus on solutions. What would Dad do?

He worked his way back to sitting up against the wall, then caterpillar-inched his way down the side of the building. It could only help to know the size of the place and perhaps find a door or a window. If there was a window—or a door. Was it possible to have a room with no door?

Whoa. Now he was having crazy thoughts. Maybe a rest would help. He was sleepy anyway. Might as well relax for a minute.

«»

His eyelids popped open. Must have fallen asleep. It was still warm, but it didn't feel as hot. Maybe things were cooling down outside.

He wiggled around. Still zip-tied. Ugh, head still hurt too. His tongue stuck to the roof of his bone-dry mouth. With effort, he peeled his tongue free and coughed. The need for water was becoming critical. His clothes held enough perspiration to fill a glass. That much fluid coming off a body had to be replaced.

Dad taught him survival skills. "You're too smart to coddle, son. Prepare for the worst, and it may save your life."

Dad had known unprepared people who ended up dead.

Dead. Caleb shivered. That better not be him soon. Why would someone lock him up in this sweatbox? And again, who?

Think, Caleb, think. What happened after the auction? Emma was there. They were going to celebrate the excellent earnings. Something small, since neither of them had money to buy something frivolous.

Puppies. That was it. Emma knew someone who had puppies for sale, and they were going to go look at them. She loved animals and couldn't wait to show him the litter. The dealer was at the far end of the market. Odd for a dealer to put himself so far away from the crowd. The closer you were to the center, the better your business was. People didn't like to walk in the heat.

He squirmed back up to a sitting position. The movement made his head swim and the room spin. At least it felt like it was spinning. It was hard to stay spatially oriented in nothing but blackness.

Emma had taken his hand as they neared the end of the market area. Sure, she was just playing and having fun, but it felt wonderful. She grinned that beautiful smile and pulled him along. He'd have gone anywhere with her right then.

At the end of the market, she pointed out the dog breeder's van. She'd said the man couldn't afford a table spot and had the puppies on the vehicle's other side. As they ran around the van, the side door slid open. But there weren't any puppies.

He stiffened now. Someone hit him on the head from behind! He'd fallen to his knees and saw Emma standing over him. She wasn't smiling now. With her hands on her hips, she smirked.

Nothing else lingered in his memory. Until he woke up in this room—this sweatbox of darkness.

His tongue stuck to the roof of his mouth again. It felt too big to be between his teeth anymore. Or maybe his mouth was shrinking in the heat. Could a mouth shrink?

Maybe another nap.

No! He'd already slept enough.

Emma wasn't a nice person. He'd been an idiot and let a girl lead him into a trap. Dad wouldn't be happy when Caleb confessed. What was lesson number one? Always be alert to your surroundings. And lesson number two? Know who your friends are.

Well, Emma, you are off the friends list. I hope you're happy.

How was he going to get out of this mess? He didn't even know how long he'd been here or where here was. *Think, Caleb, think!*

Voices rumbled outside the building. They were getting louder, closer. What should he do? Call for help? Who knew if they were the good guys or the bad guys? If he called out and they were the ones who put him here, they'd know he was awake. He'd lose any advantage surprise could bring.

But if they weren't who put him in here, this might be his only chance to break free. A rattling sound, like a chain being moved outside the building, decided for him. They were unlocking a door somewhere, not passing by.

Bad guys.

The End

Dear reader, thank you so much for sharing Jan's journey with me! If you enjoyed reading *Collapse*, I would gratefully appreciate you leaving a review on Bookbub, Goodreads, or other sites to help others discover my books. Those minutes of your time make a tremendous difference to writers like me, not only in helping others find our books but also in encouraging us to keep up the effort of writing.

And with that thought, I hope you will enjoy Caleb's story, the next tale in this series, *Honor*.

I'd love to have you join *my* posse of friends! Join my newsletter at www.AngelaDShelton.com and receive a **free** copy of my novella *Downfall*. You can also connect with me on Facebook, Instagram, Twitter, and Pinterest.

See you next time!
Angela